BIG HONEY DOG MYSTERIES
CURSE OF THE SCARAB

H.Y. HANNA

Libraries Australia Cataloguing in Publication:
Title: Curse of the Scarab/ H.Y. Hanna (Series: Big Honey Dog Mysteries; 1)
ISBN-13: 978-0-9923153-1-3; Hanna, H.Y., (author.)
Published [Perth, Western Australia] H.Y. Hanna, 2013.
ID: 52578002 ; Dewey Number: A823.4

Author's Note
This book follows British English conventions in spelling and usage.

Cover Design and Interior Format by The Killion Group
http://thekilliongroupinc.com

DEDICATION

To the real 'Big Honey Dog', who not only inspired this book but also changed my life completely—from arriving in my arms as an enormous puppy to growing up into the dog of my dreams.

And to Paul, for showing me what being a hero really means.

COLLECT THE OTHER BOOKS IN THIS SERIES:

TABLE OF CONTENTS

CHAPTER 1

Something thudded outside the front door. Honey the Great Dane raised her head, blinking in the afternoon sun that streamed in through the windows. She pricked her ears and listened.

Nothing. Perhaps she had been dreaming. She stretched luxuriously, extending every toe, and yawned. A fly buzzed along the windowsill, but otherwise the house was quiet. She sighed contentedly. Her eyelids drooped.

That sound again. A faint scuffling, outside the front door. Then voices.

Who's there? Honey sprang up with her big, booming bark, just as her human, Olivia, rushed into the room. She smiled at Honey as she headed for the front door.

"Hey, Honey... have I got a surprise for you!" Olivia said.

Ooh, a surprise? Honey wagged her tail and followed Olivia to the front door, pushing past her eagerly to see. The door swung open.

Honey stared.

A strange woman stood on the doormat,

but that wasn't who Honey was staring at. Sitting next to her was an enormous puppy. A Great Dane puppy with huge, knuckly paws, big ears flopping on either side of a chubby little face, and wrinkles across its forehead.

"Mama?" The puppy bounced up and wriggled like a happy worm. It ran towards Honey and tripped on the doormat. Picking itself up, the puppy jumped into Honey's face, panting milky puppy breath everywhere.

Ugh! Honey staggered backwards, stumbling over the puppy, and they fell together in a tangle of legs and paws.

"Aw... aren't they gorgeous together?" Olivia cooed. "Look at them! Best friends already."

Honey pulled her head out from under the puppy's bum and gaped at Olivia. *What? She knew humans could be slow sometimes, but... had Olivia lost her tennis balls?*

"This is great." Olivia smiled at the strange woman. "I'm sure Honey will be much happier with a pet sitter while I'm away, rather than going into a kennel—especially now that she has little Bean as a playmate! I hope you and Bean will enjoy staying here."

Staying here? Honey stared in horror. *What did she mean, staying here? I'm an Only Dog, thank you very much! I'm certainly not sharing my home with a puppy!*

"Bean looks just like you did at ten weeks." Olivia chuckled, fondling Honey's ears. "In fact, I think your paws were even bigger! Let's hope she doesn't end up a monster drooler like you, though." She smiled. "Aw, I can just see you two cuddling up to sleep together."

No way. Honey snorted. That pup was definitely not coming on her bed. And she was definitely not—

Oomph! Honey staggered again as something hit her, smacking her head against the hall table.

"Mama!" The puppy bounced around.

"I'm not your mama," Honey growled. "*Ow!* Stop it! That hurts." She jerked back as Bean grabbed her jowls with sharp puppy teeth.

Then the puppy saw Honey's tail. She let go of Honey's jowls and pounced on her tail instead. "Yummy!"

"No, not yummy," Honey said hastily, pulling her tail out of the way. "That's my tail."

"Tail?"

"Yes, you have one too—look." Honey nudged the little one's behind.

The puppy turned, saw her own tail, and bounced with delight. "Yummy!" And started chasing her own tail in a circle.

Honey looked at her human beseechingly. *You can't seriously be leaving me with this!* But Olivia just laughed as she watched Bean with that silly look humans get on their faces when they think something is *"adorable"*.

"Well, I must dash or I'll be late for my train," Olivia said, grabbing her bags and turning to give Honey a final pat.

No! Honey put on her best Sad Dog Eyes and whined.

Olivia looked solemnly at Honey. "Don't be silly now. Be a good girl and look after Bean. I'm counting on you." She kissed Honey's nose. "Bye!"

The door slammed after her.

Honey looked around in dismay. The Pet Sitter had gone into the kitchen, leaving her alone with the puppy, who was now trying to eat the couch. There was a horrible ripping sound as Bean chewed through the outer cover.

"No, no—don't do that!" Honey cried.

Bean stopped and looked up at her. "Why?"

"Um... because we shouldn't chew the furniture."

"Why?"

"Because... because good doggies don't chew the furniture," Honey said. "You want to be a good doggie, don't you?"

"Why?"

"Because... oh, *ticks*!" Honey took a deep breath. "Look, just wait there, OK? I'll get you something you can chew!" She hurried into the study, looking wildly around for a toy. Any toy. *Ah—there!* Under the desk. An old rubber bone. That would do. She grabbed it and hurried back into the living room, then stopped in her tracks. *What was that awful smell?*

"I poo!" Bean said proudly.

"*What?*" Honey stared in horror at the big pile of squishy, brown poo on the carpet. "No, no, Bean! You mustn't poo in the house!"

"Why?"

"Because... because... You just mustn't,

that's why," Honey said. "All doggies must only poo outside. In the garden or in the park. But never in the house. Do you understand?"

Bean looked puzzled. "Wee-wee too?"

"Yes, wee-wee too," Honey said firmly. "All outside. Only outside." She looked worriedly at Bean. "Do you want to do a wee-wee now?"

Bean bounced. "Yes! Wee-wee now!"

"OK, OK! Just hold it," Honey said desperately as she turned and ran into the kitchen. The Pet Sitter was standing by the kettle, fussing with a cup and spoon. Honey rushed over and nudged her. The woman looked at her blankly. Honey nudged her again, then walked to the doorway of the kitchen and looked back. The woman grinned and turned back to the kettle.

Oh, for barking out loud! Honey gritted her teeth. What dog could pull off a Lassie when you had such a dumb human to work with?

She went back and whined again, pleading with her eyes. It took her five long minutes before the Pet Sitter understood what she wanted, and by the time they came back into the hallway, there was a little yellow puddle next to the poo.

"Oh, Bean!" The Pet Sitter gasped. "You naughty pup! You *bad girl!*"

The Great Dane puppy looked up with big, scared eyes. Hunching over and making herself as small as she could, Bean crept to a corner of the room, hanging her head. Honey watched as the Pet Sitter cleaned up the mess and stomped back to the kitchen.

It was quiet now. No puppy bouncing in her face, no puppy teeth nipping her skin, no puppy squeals in her ears. *How nice to have peace again!* Honey told herself. She climbed on her bed and resolutely shut her eyes. But sleep wouldn't come. Her mind kept straying back to that little shape huddled in the corner.

Honey raised her head and looked over at Bean. It was none of her business, really. The puppy *had* been bad and should have been told off. Every dog knows you mustn't toilet in the house. Still, Bean did look so little and scared.

Honey got up and went over to the puppy. Bean peeked at her and whispered, "Me bad girl?"

Honey hesitated, then gave the top of the puppy's head a quick lick. "No... it was an accident."

The puppy looked down at her paws again, the wrinkles furrowing even deeper on her brow.

Honey tried again. "Er... do you want my chew bone?"

The puppy's only response was to sink even lower. Honey looked back at her bed, then at the puppy. She gave her head a shake. *I don't believe I'm doing this.* She nudged the puppy gently with her nose. "Would you like to come on my bed with me?"

Bean brightened and gave a little bounce. It was just a small one, but Honey felt her heart warm. She led the puppy back to her bed and settled back in the middle. Bean snuggled close against her belly. A faint rumble of little snores soon filled the air. Honey looked down at the soft bundle next to her, at the oversized ears and the huge baby paws.

She's rather cute, Honey thought with surprise. Gently, she lowered her head down, curving her neck around Bean. It was strange sharing her bed, she thought, shifting around—she wasn't sure she liked it. Still, she didn't want to disturb the puppy, so she would just lie here a bit longer. There was no way, though, that she would fall asleep…

Honey was woken by a thump. She jerked her head up. The space next to her was empty.

Bean?

She sprang off the bed, sniffing anxiously for the puppy's scent. Then she stopped in relief. Bean was sitting by the front door, waiting while a leash was clipped onto her collar. The Pet Sitter held up Honey's leash too and smiled.

"Come along, Honey! Time for your walk!"

It was late afternoon—the time when most dogs like to walk their humans—and the streets were full of canines busily leading the way to the park. As they rounded the corner, Honey caught sight of Ruffster, the mongrel mutt who lived down the street. He was his usual scruffy self, his fur sticking up in odd places and one ear up, one ear down. He wagged his tail as soon as he saw her and dragged his hapless owner over to join them.

"You heard the news, mate?" He panted as they fell into step beside each other.

"What news?" Honey furrowed her brow. "You mean about the new pet store?"

"Nah, mate! There's some pups gone missin'. That Golden Retriever who lives on the other side of the cemetery—lovely girl, I knew her mother—anyway, her first litter it was, ready to go to their new homes and all, but when they checked this mornin'... All gone! Real state she was in. Her people are puttin' up posters everywhere." Ruffster sat down and scratched his upright ear. "Who's that little tyke? Your family got a new pup too?"

Honey swung around and saw Bean, who was trying to eat a lamp post.

"Oh no," said Honey hastily, "she belongs to my Pet Sitter. They're just staying at my house while my human is away."

"Better keep an eye on her," Ruffster said as they all walked into the park together. "Somethin' weird's going on. I feel it in my tail."

The humans unclipped their leashes as they entered the park and Ruffster trotted ahead towards the pond with Bean scampering beside him to keep up. Honey followed more sedately, pausing to check Peemail on a few bushes along the way. But before she could do more than give a cursory sniff, she heard Ruffster calling her name. She looked up, then hurried over to join him and the group of dogs milling around the pond. Something was wrong. Usually there would have been a flurry of bum-sniffing and tail-wagging, but today everybody stood in a worried silence.

Ruffster looked at her grimly. "More pups have gone missin'. Two from those houses by the river and three from the pet store."

Honey stared at him, then at the other dogs. "Maybe the humans...?"

"Nah, it's not the humans. They're all real upset too." Ruffster prodded something on the ground with his paw. "Look—they found one o' these left behind every time pups went missin'."

Honey leaned down and sniffed carefully. It seemed to be a big black beetle with a hard, shiny shell. Stiff and dead now, with its legs curled close to its body, it gave off a sickly-sweet scent. "What is it?" She cocked her head.

"I've seen something like it!" A dog spoke up. It was Suka the Siberian Husky, her blue eyes bright with excitement. "When I was helping my Boy with his homework—one of his books from school has a picture that looks just like this. It comes from a faraway place called Egypt. It's a *scarab* and it means death."

CHAPTER 2

"Death? Who's going to die?"

"Did somebody say death?"

"Are the puppies dead?"

The panicked whispers skittered across the group of dogs like fleas on a rampage. Honey saw Bean listening with her eyes wide. The puppy was starting to look scared again.

"Nobody is going to die," Honey said quickly. "It's just a stupid, dried-up old bug, that's all." She gave Suka a sceptical look. The Husky was always full of the latest news and gossip, but sometimes her imagination could be as fluffy as her big, plumed tail. Like the time she told everyone there was a monster living in the sewer tunnels and it turned out to be just a family of rats. Or when she said the vet was making a FrankenMutt in the back room and it was just an old Dalmatian with a bandaged tail.

"It doesn't really mean death, does it?" Honey asked Suka.

"Well... not exactly," Suka admitted. "It says in my Boy's book that scarabs are also called dung beetles and the humans in Old Egypt put them all around their dead when they buried them. They thought the beetles were, like, guardians of the Underworld or something."

"Forget the stupid bugs. What about him?" growled Tyson the Jack Russell Terrier. Everyone edged out of his way. When it came to Tyson his bark was bad enough, never mind his bite. Honey had seen the gruff terrier reduce a police dog to quivering jelly once. He wrinkled his muzzle as if at a bad smell and threw a dark look over his shoulder. "I'll bet ya *he's* got something to do with it."

They all followed Tyson's gaze to where an old man sat reading a newspaper on a bench, a lone dog beside him. The sun was behind them so it was hard to make out more than a silhouette, but Honey could see muscles rippling beneath the dog's black coat and a short, grizzled muzzle.

"Who's that?" Honey asked.

"That's Max, my new neighbour," Suka said, her fluffy tail waving with excitement. She lowered her voice. "He's a *Pit Bull*."

Several dogs took a step back; others looked at each other and nodded meaningfully.

"I heard Max used to be a fighting dog," said Suka. "He was a total killer in the ring! He could take on dogs twice his size and finish them in five minutes."

"Really?" Honey glanced back at the Pit Bull.

"Festering fleas, Honey—don't ya know *any*thing?" growled Tyson. "Pit Bulls are dangerous! Everyone says so. Ya can't trust them."

"You should have seen the fuss my Boy's Mother made when she heard he was moving into our neighbourhood." Suka paused before adding in a loud whisper, "She wanted him *muzzled*."

"Muzzled!" Honey gasped. "But why?"

Suka gave a delicious shiver. "She said all Pit Bulls are vicious. I mean, he might try to kill us in our sleep or something!"

Honey frowned but before she could reply, they heard a guttural growl in the distance. She turned to look. Max was standing stiff, hackles up, staring at a dog who had just entered the park with a man. As they approached the bench, Max suddenly exploded in a frenzy of foam and snarling teeth, lunging at the new dog, who yelped and cowered away. The old man dropped his newspaper and grabbed Max around the neck while the new dog and his human hurried past.

"Did you see that?" Suka said excitedly.

"Told ya he was dangerous," Tyson growled, pushing past Honey to get a better view. A long string of drool fell from her jowls and plopped onto his head. "Aarrghh-grrrr!" spluttered Tyson.

"Oh, sorry!" Honey gulped. "That just happens sometimes—"

"Sometimes?" Ruffster laughed. "Mate, you drool *all* the time."

Tyson growled and started shaking his head from side to side, trying to fling off the slimy slobber. Bean bounced over and watched him with interest.

"Me drool too!" she said eagerly, then gave a little hiccup and regurgitated some milky liquid onto Tyson's paws.

"Bean!" Honey said, horrified. "What are you doing?"

The other dogs sniggered. Honey looked around the park, but she couldn't see the Pet Sitter anywhere. Typical. Humans were never around when you needed them. She tried to grab the puppy by the scruff but before she could get near, Bean darted away and ran off.

Honey turned back to Tyson. "Sorry! Here, let me lick that off—"

"No thanks. Keep yer dribbly jowls away from me," Tyson growled, backing up quickly. He bumped into another dog and turned in surprise. It was the new dog who had been attacked by Max.

Everyone eyed the newcomer curiously. He was a medium-sized dog with a narrow snout and pointed ears that stretched, bat-like, above his head. His black coat was smooth with an iridescent sheen, and his tail curled low behind him. Around his neck, he wore a thick, gold collar. But the most striking thing about him was his piercing yellow eyes with pupils so narrow they looked almost like slits.

Honey realised she was staring. Hastily, she dropped her eyes and found herself looking at the stranger's front paws. She blinked, wondering if she was seeing right....

"You all right, mate?" Ruffster asked. "Saw what happened with that Pit Bull."

"Yesss." The new dog had a soft, whispery voice. He shivered. "I think he wanted to kill me."

"Did he bite you?" asked Suka eagerly. "They say a Pit Bull's jaws can go right through your head!" She sidled up to the strange dog. "You're new, aren't you? I haven't seen you before and I know all the dogs in town."

"Yesss, I came recently. I am called Newbie."

"Newbie?" Ruffster laughed. "Mate, I've heard a lot o' stupid names, but that one takes the dog biscuit!" He trotted over and circled Newbie, sniffing his bum politely. "So what kind o' dog are you, anyway? I'm a Welsh Corgi with a bit o' Airedale on my mother's side; my father—they're not so sure—they reckon a bit o' Collie, definitely some Terrier and maybe even—"

Bean bounced suddenly into their midst, chasing a leaf blowing in the wind. She lunged at the leaf, tripped and fell over, smacking into the new dog.

"Bean!" Honey groaned as the puppy scrambled to her feet, jamming one paw into Newbie's face.

"It is all right." Newbie winced as the puppy stepped on his tail. "I like puppiesss." He watched as Bean bounced away again. "How old is your little sissster?"

"She's not my sister." Honey sighed. "Um,

she's about ten weeks, I think."

Newbie's eyes gleamed. "Really? She looks so big."

"Dane pups grow a lot faster than other dogs," Honey explained. "We look like a grown-up dog by four months, but we're really still big babies and—" She stopped suddenly as she realised Bean was bouncing towards the bench where Max and the old man were sitting.

"Wait—Bean!" she cried in horror.

Too late. The puppy bounced right up to the bench and crashed into Max's back. The Pit Bull turned in surprise. Bean tumbled over and landed on her back, her huge paws splayed in all directions as she looked up at him with big, scared eyes.

Max sprang up and moved towards the puppy.

"Leave her alone!" Honey yelped. She charged over and flung herself over Bean's body, turning to face the Pit Bull with bared teeth. "She's only a baby!"

Up close, Max was every bit as frightening as Suka had suggested: long, pitted scars snaked across his face and one eyelid drooped, the eyeball red and bloodshot. His body was covered with more scars, and between the bulging muscles showed areas where the fur had not grown back around the puckered, damaged skin.

Honey shuddered in spite of herself and knew that he could smell her fear. She said a bit wildly, "Don't... don't you touch her!"

"What did you think I was going to do?"

Honey stopped short. His voice was deep and guttural but not as harsh as she had expected. And it must have been a trick of the afternoon sun, but for a moment, she thought it was sadness—not madness—that she saw in his eyes.

"I…" She hesitated, then glanced back at her friends. They were watching avidly. She knew what they were thinking: *Honey, the big, useless lump…*

She turned back to Max. "You're a Pit Bull, aren't you?" she snarled. "That's all I need to know!"

Max stiffened and his eyes went hard. Honey braced herself, but the Pit Bull just gave a deep growl in his throat and turned away. "Keep that pup away from me."

Honey watched him warily for a moment, then nudged Bean quickly to her feet. As they walked back to the other dogs, Bean sneaked a look back at Max.

"Doggie scary."

"Yes, doggie scary," Honey agreed. "You keep away from that doggie, you understand?"

Bean nodded and scampered off. The other dogs surrounded Honey eagerly as she rejoined them.

"Did you see his fangs? Does he smell?" Suka asked.

"Holy liver treat, mate," said Ruffster. "That was somethin' else! "

"Proud of ya, Honey," growled Tyson. "Never thought ya had it in ya."

"It wasn't like that…" Honey protested.

But nobody was listening. They were all jostling around her, wagging their tails. Honey had never been the centre of so much admiration before. She should have been enjoying the moment, but all she could think about was the look in Max's eyes when she had snarled at him.

She turned hastily to Ruffster. "Where's the new dog?"

"Went off," said Ruffster. "Bit o' an odd mutt, don't you think? Stupid name. And he talks really funny."

"Maybe he can't help it," said Honey. "Some dogs are born... you know, a bit different."

"Yeah, I guess. I knew this mutt who barked like a squeakin' hinge." Ruffster cocked his leg against a park bin. "Think I'm headin' home. See my Guy over there callin' me."

They all heard a voice shrieking Suka's name.

"Howling hyenas, listen to my Boy's Mother screeching." Suka sighed. "When is she ever going to learn that calling me once is enough? Huskies will come when they're ready!"

"Yeah, some humans are really hard to train," agreed Ruffster. "My Guy ain't too bad. Problem I have is teachin' him to share. Managed with the couch, though, so I'm makin' progress. Just got to be consistent."

They heard Suka's name being screamed again.

"Uh-oh, better go." Suka grinned as they

saw a woman stomping, red-faced, in their direction. "Are you bringing that pup tomorrow, Honey?"

"Yes, I guess so. She's staying with..." Honey glanced around. "Where is she?"

Bean was nowhere to be seen. In the distance, Honey could see the Pet Sitter walking around, a worried expression on her face.

"Bean? Bean?" The Pet Sitter cupped her hands around her mouth. "BEAN!"

Something in her voice made the hairs on Honey's neck stand up.

"Has anyone seen her?" Honey whirled around to the other dogs. They all looked blank. "She was here with me just a moment ago!" Honey insisted.

Everyone put their noses to the ground. Honey ran in circles, sniffing urgently. Nothing. Not one whiff of a scent. It was as if the puppy had just vanished.

Then she stopped short, staring at something on the ground. It was the leaf Bean had been chasing. It was wedged against something else.

Something black.

The dead scarab beetle Ruffster had shown her earlier.

"Hey, mate," said Ruffster, coming up slowly behind her and staring at the scarab too. "You don't reckon this is like those other pups that've gone missin'?"

Honey felt her heart lurch in her chest. *No... surely it was a coincidence?*

"Ya should ask that Pit Bull," growled

Tyson.

Honey turned quickly, but the park bench was empty. Max was gone.

CHAPTER 3

Honey's heart pounded in time to her paws as she raced along the path in the park, straining her eyes to see into the gathering darkness. The sun was setting now and shadows were creeping long across the grass, merging with the black silhouettes of the trees and bushes around them.

"Mate, you don't reckon the pup came this far?" Ruffster said as they skidded to a stop on the far side of the park. 'C'mon—she's only ten weeks old!"

"I don't know... but we've got to look, haven't we?" Honey panted, drool dripping from her jowls. "Maybe she got lost. Maybe she was following someone... I don't understand—she was with me just a moment ago... I know she was there!"

Behind them, they could still faintly hear the Pet Sitter by the pond, calling for Bean. A few other human voices rose with hers—some of the other dog owners must have joined in to help.

"Should we look near the playground?

And what about the toilets—do you think she might be in there?" Honey paced in a circle.

"Wait… that's Biscuit the Beagle's house," said Ruffster, looking over the bushes to a house across the road. "C'mon, let's get him to help us search. If *he* can't pick up her scent, nobody can."

The leader of the Beagle Brigade was famous for having the best nose in town. He was also famous for eating anything and everything. Legend had it that Biscuit once chowed down an entire TV remote and burped up the plastic buttons. He looked up from a hole he was digging as they approached his garden fence and said hopefully, "Got anything to eat?"

Honey gave an apologetic wag. "No, sorry. But—"

The Beagle gave a mournful howl. "I'm going to starve to death."

"Don't your humans feed you?" Ruffster asked.

"Yes, but that was this morning," Biscuit protested. "And they still haven't come home yet. Who knows when I'm going to get my dinner? Besides, they never give me enough. They're always talking about a diet or something. I mean, do I look fat to you?"

Honey eyed the Beagle's podgy belly. "Er… well—"

"Anyway," Biscuit went on, "I managed to find a few tasty things in the living room this morning. The Missus left her handbag on the coffee table so I had a good rummage around. Found a couple of mints, some rubber bands, a lip balm—mm, strawberry flavour, my favourite, had two of those already—oh, and this little rectangular thing with a nice chewy cover. Took me a while to get my teeth into it. Think it's that thing the Missus holds up to her ear all the time—"

"Mate, you didn't eat her iBone?" said Ruffster, aghast.

"What's that?"

"It's, like, one of the humans' favourite toys! They carry it around with them all the time and poke it with their hands. It's always makin' noises. You didn't really eat it?"

"Just half of it." Biscuit licked his lips. "It was all right, a bit metallic. I was just getting to the bits inside when my Missus came in the room. So I swallowed as much as I could and pushed the rest under the sofa. Don't think she'll find it. She was going around all morning, looking behind cushions and—"

"Biscuit, listen!" Honey cut in. "We're looking for a puppy who's gone missing. Her name is Bean; she was staying with me. Please, can you help?"

Biscuit's ears perked up with interest. "Missing Pawson, eh? I specialise in those. Got anything with her scent on it?"

"Try this," Ruffster said, reaching up to snag something from Honey's jowls. It was the leaf Bean had been chasing earlier. It had stuck to the drool on Honey's chin when she sniffed it and she'd carried it around with them. Ruffster dropped it over the garden fence. Biscuit stuck his nose into the leaf and sniffed intently. Then he stood up tall and raised his head, scenting the air.

"Mm... yes..." He closed his eyes, breathing deeply. "Yes... I'm picking up something...." He opened his eyes, his tail wagging. "Yes! *A-woo-woo-woo!* A scent! A scent! Come on, I've got to get tracking."

Ruffster looked at the fence sceptically. "But how're you goin' to do that? Thought you said your folks reinforced the fence after your last escape?"

"Oh yeah." Biscuit chuckled. "But nobody can keep a Beagle in. There's a gap at the back I think I can squeeze through. I'll meet you dogs in a minute." He turned and disappeared around the back of his house.

A few minutes later they were back in the park, watching Biscuit as he ran around in circles, pausing, sniffing, rushing ahead, pausing again, casting around, then running off in a new direction. He hovered around the pond, then turned suddenly towards the side entrance of the park. He rushed towards the bench Max and the old man were sitting on earlier.

The others followed eagerly. Biscuit plunged his nose under the bench. He came up with a greasy wrapper smeared with mayonnaise, which he proceeded to eat, paper and all.

"Biscuit!" Ruffster groaned. "You're supposed to be lookin' for a lost puppy, not your dinner!"

"Sorry." Biscuit licked some mayonnaise off his nose. "This was simply too good to pass up. Mm... must be from that new deli in town. I must tell the other Beagle Brigade members and—"

"Biscuit!"

"OK, OK," the Beagle grumbled. "Just let me leave them a Peemail." He cocked his leg against the bench, then turned in a circle and put his nose to the ground once more.

Honey glanced back towards the pond. She couldn't see the Pet Sitter anymore, although she could still faintly hear voices calling Bean's name in the distance. The humans must have moved to the other side of the park to search for Bean. Most of the other dogs had left and the grass by the pond was deserted except for a lone dog hurrying over to join them.

It was Tyson the Jack Russell. He shook his head as he met Honey's eyes. "Nothing."

There was a sneeze beside her. Honey turned back to Biscuit, who was standing rigid, his nose twitching. The next minute, he gave another *A-woo-woo-woo!* and rushed out of the park, his nose along the ground. The other dogs hesitated, then followed him across the street.

Twilight had come, sinking most of the street in darkness except for the fuzzy pools of yellow light around each lamp post. The houses loomed up on either side of the road. Biscuit trotted past a few doors, then turned into Lemon Tree Lane, which led away from the park. He didn't stop until he reached the last house at the bottom of the lane. Beyond it, the dogs could see the gnarled, old oak trees of the cemetery, sharp against an indigo sky.

Biscuit ran back and forth in front of the house, his nose along the ground, making snuffling noises. "Here!" He panted. "She's here! Here!"

CHAPTER 4

Honey stared up at the house, her hackles rising. A solid wood gate faced the street, its blank façade giving nothing away, and on either side stretched a high hedge. Behind it, the house brooded, its faded, brick walls laced with creeping ivy.

Honey hesitated, then stepped up to the gate. She nudged it with her nose. It creaked slightly but did not open.

"How about tryin' the back?" whispered Ruffster.

They followed the high hedge along the front of the house to where it ended in a sharp corner just before it met the stone wall of the cemetery. The dogs peered around the corner of the shrubbery. A narrow passageway showed between the hedgerow and the cemetery wall, which converged into blackness.

"This must lead to the back o' the house," Ruffster said.

Honey gently pushed past the others and stepped into the narrow space. "I'll go first."

The rest followed her, one by one, and they shuffled slowly down the passageway. As they went deeper, the light from the lane behind them dimmed and Honey found herself groping for each step with her front paws. Finally, she began to see a lessening of the darkness ahead of her. She quickened her steps and came out into a small alley that ran along the back of the houses.

The other dogs spilled out of the passageway behind her and looked warily around. It seemed deserted. Farther down the alley stood two big plastic bins on wheels. Biscuit's nose twitched as he looked at them with sudden interest. Honey raised her nose in the same direction and caught the rich, fetid scent of fresh rubbish.

"Garbage gourmet!" Biscuit's tail began to wag, his eyes bright with anticipation. He bustled towards the bins, then sprang back in surprise as a ferocious yowl rent the air and a black shape sprang out from the shadows behind one of the bins.

"Yikes!" Biscuit scrambled backwards. He fell over as the black cat swiped a paw at him and hissed, its fur puffed into a coat of hedgehog spikes.

Honey cringed away but Ruffster rushed forwards, barking excitedly. The cat spat and hissed again, lunging forwards to rake its claws across Ruffster's face. Ruffster jerked back just in time, but before he could do anything else, the cat turned and shot up the wall behind the bins. It perched at the top to spit at Ruffster again and give him Kitty Evil

Eye.

"You say that to my face, you pathetic meow-sack!" yelled Ruffster, jumping up after the cat. It gave him a disdainful glare, then turned and disappeared over the wall, out of sight.

Biscuit stood up and gave himself a shake. "I thought I was going to be cat food for a moment! I've never met a cat that scary. The ones on my street always run away when they see me."

"All cats are scary," said Honey with a shudder.

"That was no fat pet kitty," said Ruffster with authority. "That was a feral."

"A f...feral?" Honey looked at the wall over which the black cat had disappeared. "But where do they come from?"

"Suka told me there's a feral cat colony on the other side of the cemetery," said Biscuit. "She says the cats there are ferocious—they have fangs that hang out of their mouths and eyes that glow in the dark—"

"How would she know, mate?" Ruffster scoffed. "She been there herself?"

"Oh, no. Suka says nobody who visits the feral cat colony ever comes out alive," said Biscuit.

Tyson rolled his eyes and growled, "Well, she's right about cats being unbalanced. I know. I live with one."

"Come on, we're wasting time," said Honey, turning back towards the hedge.

Biscuit gave the bins a wistful look, then sighed and followed her. They clustered around the hedge. It wasn't as high as at the front of the house, but even so, Honey was the only dog tall enough to see over its clipped edges.

"What do you see, Honey?"

Honey stood up as high as she could on her tiptoes, peering through the gloom of the garden inside and towards the house. The back windows were lit and in the pale orange glow, she could make out what looked like a kitchen. On the floor beside the kitchen counter was a dog bed and two bowls. The bed was empty.

"Honey! What do you see?"

"Can you see the pup?"

"Is there any food?" Biscuit asked.

Honey shook her head. "I don't see anyone. The kitchen's empty. I can't see into the rest of the house, though—maybe Bean is in another room or... Oh, I wish we could get closer." She growled in frustration.

"Hey! Reckon we can— Look, here's a gap." Ruffster nosed the bottom of the hedge. There was certainly a patch where the leaves had thinned out and the hedge had parted slightly to reveal a small hollow.

Honey looked at the gap doubtfully. "Well, for you smaller dogs maybe. But for me..."

"No problem... Just need to dig under a bit, widen the hole up," Ruffster said, starting to paw at the loose soil around the gap.

"Out of the way! This is a job for a terrier!" Tyson growled, pushing past Ruffster and throwing himself at the gap. Nobody could dig a hole like Tyson. He ploughed through the earth with his front paws, raking up roots and stones and throwing enormous clumps of soil out behind him. In a few moments, all you could see of Tyson was his rump and his tail as his head and shoulders burrowed out of sight and into the tunnel he had made.

"Wow," Ruffster muttered under his breath. "Never thought such a small dog could dig such a big hole so fast."

"Who ya calling small?" Tyson growled, backing out of the hole and shaking himself. He turned to Honey. "Go on, try it."

Honey crouched down and stuck her head and shoulders into the hole, crawling forwards on her belly. The moist smell of fresh earth filled her nose. Loose soil crumbled and rained down into her eyes and she could feel stones scraping the skin of her belly, but she pushed forwards. Then her shoulders jammed against something hard— a root maybe—and she stuck fast. She pushed and struggled but nothing budged. She tried to squirm backwards, back out of the hole, but found that she couldn't move that way either. All around her, the earth pressed down. Honey felt panic rise in her throat.

An earthworm wriggled near her nose, causing her to jerk back in surprise. More soil crumbled around her, but she felt something shift by her right shoulder. She threw herself forwards again, scrabbling and struggling anew. With a frantic scraping of her back paws, she pushed her way out of the hole.

She stood up, panting. She was in.

CHAPTER 5

Honey looked around, straining her eyes to see in the dim light. Trees crowded the backyard, their branches spreading like ragged umbrellas above her head. Weeds lined the path leading up to the house and bushes grew wild and tangled everywhere.

A scrabbling of paws sounded behind her and Honey turned to find Ruffster shaking himself as he emerged from the hole, followed by Biscuit and Tyson. Hugging the shadows, they crept along the path towards the house and huddled under the kitchen window. It was open slightly. Honey reached up and shoved her nose through the gap, trying to push it further ajar, but all she managed to do was leave a smear of drool on the windowpane.

She turned back to the others with a sigh. "I can't get it open wider."

"Tyson, mate, you should be able to get through there," said Ruffster. "You're small enough... *Er...*" He paused as the Jack Russell glared at him. "I mean, you've got the special skills."

Tyson gave a grunt, then jumped up onto the ledge outside the kitchen window. He stuck his head into the gap and wriggled forwards. The others held their breath as he was wedged tight for a moment, his body half in and half out of the kitchen. Then, with another wriggle, he was through. He landed on the kitchen counter which ran under the window. Everybody breathed again.

Tyson paused, his ears pricked, listening. They all listened. There were some muffled sounds coming from the second storey but no footsteps on the stairs. So far, so good. Tyson began inching his way along the counter.

"Careful you don't fall in that sink, mate," Ruffster hissed.

"Can you pick up Bean's scent?" Honey called.

"Do you see any food?" Biscuit asked, jumping onto the outside window ledge himself and sticking his nose through the gap. "I think I can smell bread. Maybe they've left some on the counter?"

"Biscuit!" Ruffster growled.

"What?" Biscuit flicked his ears. "He's in there! He might as well have a look!"

Tyson tiptoed carefully around the kettle and big jars labelled COFFEE and SUGAR, hopped over the toaster, then made his way cautiously down the last stretch of counter, towards the kitchen doorway. He paused as he reached the end, his eyes fixed on something. Honey craned her neck to see what he was looking at: a bag of dog food on the floor, by the doorway. Her heartbeat quickened as she read the label. Puppy food.

Tyson gathered himself to jump off the counter. Then froze.

They all froze.

Footsteps. Coming quickly down the stairs.

"Tyson! Get out! Quick!"

Tyson darted back towards the open window, not caring now what he knocked over on his way. A utensil jar toppled over, sending spatulas, knives, and ladles clattering to the floor; the COFFEE jar spun sideways across the counter and a roll of paper towels went flying, unravelling in a quilted sheet of white across the kitchen floor.

"Hurry!"

Almost there. Tyson was almost at the gap in the window when a shape loomed in the doorway and they heard a yell of surprise.

"*What the*—?"

Tyson dived behind a row of potted herbs by the window. It must have usually been a sunny spot because the bunches of coriander, mint, and basil flourished in tall, thick clumps. Maybe they would be enough to hide him. Honey hoped so.

She ducked down with the other dogs, beneath the bottom of the window frame. All except Biscuit, who hadn't had time to jump off the ledge. He flattened his body as low as he could. With the dimness outside and the bright lights in the kitchen, he was mostly in shadow. If the man didn't turn and look that way, he might go unnoticed.

The dogs all held their breath and hoped.

Footsteps. Walking slowly around the kitchen. They heard muttering.

Honey risked a peek over the ledge. An old man had his back turned to them and was picking things up off the floor, setting them back on the counter. She could see Tyson watching the man tensely from behind the potted herbs. His body quivered as he tried to slow his panting. Outside, on her side of the window pane, Biscuit huddled as small as he could, but Honey noticed that he seemed to be shaking too.

Not in fear, though. Biscuit was having a fit of the hiccups. He shuddered as he tried to control the spasms jolting his body. "Hic!"

"Shhh! Biscuit!" hissed Ruffster. "He'll hear you!"

"*Hic!*"

"Shush!"

"*HIC!*"

The old man turned around, frowning. Tyson tried to shrink even smaller behind the herbs.

Biscuit clamped his mouth shut, his eyes panicked. He could jump off the ledge, but if he did, the movement would draw the man's attention and bring him over to the window, right next to where Tyson was hiding.

Biscuit gave another muffled "*Hic!*"

The old man looked sharply at the open window and started walking towards it.

"Ticks!" growled Tyson.

"*Hic!*" gulped Biscuit.

And then suddenly the air was shattered

by a loud musical beeping. All the dogs jumped, then stared at Biscuit, who was looking down in horror at his own stomach. From the side of his furry belly music floated out, beeping and warbling.

"Biscuit!" Ruffster groaned. "It's that iBone you swallowed, mate!"

Honey jerked her eyes back to the kitchen, expecting the old man to be looming at the window, but instead he had stopped as soon as he heard the music. A look of confusion crossed his face.

"Quick, Tyson," Honey called. "He's not looking now!"

The Jack Russell needed no further urging. He sprang up from behind the herbs and shoved himself through the gap in the window. Together, he and Biscuit nearly tumbled off the ledge as they scrambled to get back down to the ground.

They heard another yell from inside the kitchen.

"Quick! Let's get out o' here!" Ruffster shot towards the gap in the hedge.

They scurried down the path back towards the hedge, trying to keep as quiet as possible. Ruffster cast around, looking for the hole while the others threw worried looks over their shoulders.

"Found it!" Ruffster stuck his head into the hedge, wagging his tail. He pulled back and turned to Honey. "Here, mate, you go first."

Honey stepped forwards, but before she could lower her head to the hole, there was a rustle to the right and a shape exploded out of the dark.

She reeled back as something snarled in her face. She saw a muzzle covered in scars and a red, drooping eye. It was Max the Pit Bull.

"What are you doing in my garden?"

CHAPTER 6

Honey stared into the Pit Bull's furious eyes and her tail shrank under her belly, but she stood her ground.

"I...I'm looking for Bean," she explained. "You know, the little Dane pup who was with me at the—"

"She's not here," Max cut in.

"Why should we believe ya?" growled Tyson. "Her scent trail leads right into yer place and there's a bag of puppy food in yer kitchen! Why would ya have puppy food if yer not keeping a pup here?"

Max lifted his lip to show his teeth. "That's none of your business. I told you she's not here. Now get out."

"Ya think I'm scared of ya?" growled Tyson, bristling. He squared up to the Pit Bull and curled his own lips, baring his fangs.

Max snarled back and Tyson hurled himself forwards. The Jack Russell was smaller, but what he lacked in size, he made up for in ferocity and sheer, reckless courage. He lunged for Max's throat, trying to sink his teeth into the soft skin there, but the Pit Bull whipped neatly out of the way. Foam and spittle and ugly growls filled the air as they disappeared in a blur of fur and flashing teeth. Ruffster jumped up, barking frantically, while Biscuit took a step towards them, his face uncertain.

"Stop it!" Honey shouted, trying to shoulder them apart.

From the house behind them, they heard a yell and the sound of running feet, followed by something crashing. The noise seemed to get through to the fighting dogs and they fell apart, panting. Tyson had a ripped ear that was bleeding profusely, but it was Max who had several puncture wounds oozing blood on his chest and muzzle.

"Ya fight like a runty rabbit. Call yerself a fighting dog?" Tyson sneered.

Max didn't answer. Honey stared at him, at all those bulging muscles on that sinewy body and the hard glint in his eyes. She shivered. No, Max could have killed Tyson in a second if he had wanted to. The Pit Bull had been holding himself back. *But why?*

Another yell from the house galvanised them into action.

"C'mon, c'mon! Let's get out o' here!" Ruffster nudged Tyson towards the hole. The Jack Russell hesitated, his eyes on Max, then turned and wriggled into the hole, followed by Ruffster and Biscuit. Honey paused and looked at Max.

"Go," he said.

The sound of the back door opening made

up Honey's mind and she dived for the hole. Crawling through was a bit easier this time and she heaved herself out of the hole just as she heard the old man arrive on the other side of the hedge. There was an exclamation, then his voice dropped to a murmur and she heard Max whine softly in response.

"C'mon, Honey!" Ruffster called from the side passageway. "What're you waitin' for?"

She hurried after him and followed the others as they jostled and pushed their way up the passageway between the house and cemetery, back to Lemon Tree Lane at the front. Emerging cautiously, they glanced at the front gate but it looked as inscrutable as before. There was no sound from the other side of the high hedge.

"Tyson, mate—you crazy? Attackin' a Pit Bull?" Ruffster said.

"I don't trust him," Tyson growled, shaking the blood from his torn ear. "Up to no good."

"Are you all right?" asked Honey, eyeing his bloody ear in concern. "Maybe you should go to the vet—"

"I'm fine! Ya don't have to fuss over me," growled Tyson. "Ya should be thinking about the missing pup.'

"Yeah," Ruffster said. "Maybe that Old Man has all the missin' puppies inside the house somewhere. Suka reckons that humans who keep Pit Bulls are all nasty types."

Honey glanced at Biscuit who had been very quiet, not joining in the conversation. Instead, he sat with his nose twitching, looking around with a preoccupied air. Suddenly, he jumped up and began running along the outside of the high hedge, his nose to the ground, his brow furrowed in concentration.

"A mistake!" Biscuit yelped. "A mistake! A mistake!"

They all stared at him.

Biscuit shook himself, then started running in circles again, his nose back to the ground. "Her scent! Doesn't go into the house! Goes past! Goes past!"

"Chokin' chicken bones..." Ruffster groaned. "You're tellin' us this *now*? After we just nearly got eaten by the Hound o' the Baskervilles?"

Biscuit stopped and sniffed huffily. "There are a lot of confusing tracks around here. Smells like a lot of pups have been through here recently."

"So where does Bean's scent lead?" Honey asked.

Biscuit turned his head and looked towards the bottom of the lane.

"To the cemetery."

The cemetery was Honey's least favourite part of town. Her human, Olivia, had brought her here a few times for walks, thinking Honey would enjoy the chance to explore a new place, but Honey had always tried to get out again as soon as possible. She shuddered as they stepped through the rusted iron gates. The place was creepy. Tall grass grew in clumps around the headstones, making it hard to see clearly, and the old oak trees stretched their gnarled branches out like beseeching arms. Although a full moon had risen, its pale light hardly penetrated through the trees. It was so dark Honey could barely see her own paws on the cobbled pathway.

"*Ugh,*" said Biscuit, shivering as they advanced slowly down the dark path. "*T*his place has a horrible feeling."

"It's where the humans put their dead," growled Tyson.

"And some of ours too," Ruffster said, wandering off the path to look at a small stone memorial wedged into the ground. They all followed him. Carved into the smooth surface of the stone were faint words next to a line drawing of a dog with one front paw raised. There was just enough light from the moon to make out the message:

IN MEMORY OF MILO—BEST FRIEND A MAN COULD EVER HAVE. RUN FREE.

"Say, I remember Milo," said Ruffster. "I was just a pup then—he was the oldest dog on the street. Always used to pass his house on the way to puppy school. Stopped seein' him after a while... So, he's here."

Behind Milo's memorial was another marker stone... and another... and another... all bearing the names of different pets. They walked around, peering at each headstone, reading the inscriptions in hushed tones.

"This one says *OUR BELOVED BELLA— A CHAMPION IN THE RING, A*

CHAMPION IN OUR HEARTS. UNTIL WE MEET AGAIN. It's got a picture of a paw print. Do you think it's Bella the Collie who used to live across the river?" asked Honey.

Biscuit read the next marker. "*JESSIE & MERLIN—GONE BUT NEVER FORGOTTEN. THANK YOU FOR THE LAUGHTER AND THE MEMORIES*. Oh, I knew Jessie. She lived a few houses down from me. She always had the best bones. Merlin was the cat she lived with."

"They buried a cat and dog together?" said Ruffster, aghast.

"Well, not every dog hates cats as much as you do," said Biscuit. "Some dogs quite like cats."

"Look at this one…" Honey said softly. "It's got some hearts on it and says *WON-TON, OUR HANDSOME BOY—TAKEN TOO SOON. ALWAYS BY OUR SIDE, ALWAYS IN OUR HEARTS*."

"It would kill any dog to have a name like that," growled Tyson.

Ruffster cocked his head at one memorial stone that stood apart from the rest. "Can't be worse than the name on that one: *KHEPRI*. What kind o' name is that?"

He started towards the stone but was stopped by Biscuit who stiffened suddenly, his nose twitching. "Here!" he cried. "Her scent's here!"

"Bean?" Honey came forwards eagerly. "Where?"

"You sure, mate?" Ruffster said. "'Coz I don't want to be walkin' into some psycho dog den just 'coz your nose makes a mistake again—"

"Tracking is an art, not an exact science." Biscuit gave an indignant sniff. "Anyway, I told you, I got confused because there were the scents of so many other puppies."

Honey was barely listening to them. There was something in the soft soil around the memorial stones. She stooped and strained her eyes to see in the dim light. *Paw prints.* Not just one set but many different ones. Most of them were quite small. *Puppy paw prints?*

Ruffster peered over Honey's shoulder and saw the paw prints too. "Holy liver treat! Is one o' those Bean's?"

"I don't know," said Honey, lowering her head again and sniffing hopefully. But Biscuit was right. There were so many scents here, mixed together, that it was impossible to pick one out. She could definitely smell the milky scent of puppies, though.

She raised her head and looked at the prints again. They were jumbled together as if many puppies had been huddling together in the same spot. Although the soft soil showed the indentations of toes and paw pads clearly, it was still hard to distinguish individual prints.

One set, though, stood out from the rest. For one thing, they looked like adult prints, but more than that, they had a strange number of toes. Most dogs have four toes on each paw, or five sometimes if they still have their dewclaws. These prints, though, showed only three toes. Honey furrowed her brow. She knew they weren't Bean's. She remembered looking at Bean's paws as the puppy had slept next to her earlier that afternoon—was it only a few hours ago? Her heart clenched as she remembered the way the puppy had snuggled into her belly. *Where was Bean now? Was she OK?*

"Hey, these prints are leadin' off in this direction," Ruffster said excitedly, his eyes intent as he followed the paw prints. The other dogs joined him and they soon found themselves standing in front of the memorial stone with the strange name.

"D'you see what I'm seein'?" asked Ruffster in a hushed voice.

The others nodded. The soil on the other side of the memorial stone was freshly dug and raised in a shallow mound. Something had been buried here recently. Honey felt fear creep up her back like an insidious tick. She was scared to look and yet she had to know. She started towards the mound but was stopped by Ruffster's voice.

"Look! See what it says on the stone?"

Sharply etched on the memorial stone were the words:

—KHEPRI—
HE WHO DISTURBS
SHALL AWAKEN THE CURSE
BLACK HUNGER ON SKIN
CONSUME FROM WITHIN

The epitaph was followed by a series of

little pictures underneath. But they looked nothing like the pictures of hearts and paw prints on the other stones. These showed strange birds with hooked beaks and single eyes that stared with menace, crude hands and human feet and slithering snakes and squiggles.

"Curse?" Biscuit sniffed the air nervously. "What does that mean?"

Honey started forwards again, but Ruffster blocked her way. "Mate—you crazy? Didn't you read what it said?"

Honey couldn't take her eyes off the mound. "I don't care... I need to know if Bean... I need to know what's buried under there."

She pushed Ruffster out of the way and scrambled onto the mound. Ignoring the others, she started digging, her big paws raking the soft soil aside in huge sweeps. Fear churned in her stomach and dread lodged in her throat like a choking bone, but she kept on digging. Something appeared in the earth—something that gleamed. She dug faster, her breath coming in short bursts. A flash of colour, the tinkle of metal, the waxy smell of leather... The loose soil was brushed aside and Honey stood back to see what she had unearthed.

They lay in a pitiful heap, buckles rubbing, loops entwined. Pink and purple and red and blue. Soft leather and stretchy nylon. Cute cartoons and garish colours. *Puppy collars.*

"What happened to the puppies who were wearing them?" whispered Biscuit.

Ruffster glanced at Honey, who was staring fixedly at the pile. "Mate... er... d'you see...?"

Honey let out the breath she had been holding. "No, Bean's collar isn't here." She swallowed. "But Biscuit's right—what happened to *these* puppies? Where are they?"

"You reckon this could be linked to the other pups that have gone missin'?" Ruffster asked. "Let me take a closer look."

He started towards Honey, then jumped back as if he had stepped on a hot plate. The ground beside Ruffster's front paws trembled, then something shiny and black erupted from the crumbling soil.

"It's one of those dead scarabs," growled Tyson.

But as they watched, the shell suddenly moved and they saw six black legs wriggle to life.

"That ain't no dead beetle," said Ruffster, slowly backing away, his tail between his legs.

Tyson growled, his hackles raised, while Biscuit flinched backwards.

Honey looked in horror from left to right. Shiny black shapes were burrowing out of the soil all around them, clawing their way out on jointed legs covered with bristling black hairs. Each beetle had a domed head covered with a thick carapace from which a jagged mouthpart protruded. A sharp *click-click-click* sound filled the air. The soil around them roiled and vomited up more black shapes as hundreds of scarab beetles

swarmed forwards around the huddled dogs.
Click-click-click-click!
They were trapped.

CHAPTER 7

"Honey, get away from those collars!"

Honey stumbled her way across to join the other dogs. The scarabs seethed around them, filling the air with their sinister clicking. The space around the dogs began shrinking. Tyson barked and lunged at the black swarm, his teeth snapping on empty air.

"Tyson! Didn't you read the curse? *'BLACK HUNGER ON SKIN, CONSUME FROM WITHIN'*... Don't touch 'em, mate— they'll burrow into you and eat you alive or somethin'!" cried Ruffster, crowding as close as possible to Honey's body while Biscuit tried to fit himself under her belly.

Tyson reluctantly came to stand next to Honey, then shuddered as something wet and slimy fell on his shoulder. He looked up in disgust.

"Sorry, sorry!" Honey licked the dangling drool from her jowls. "I... it happens when I'm scared or stressed."

"I'll be stress-droolin' too if we don't get out o' here!" said Ruffster, his eyes on the black beetles.

Honey looked around desperately. A few meters to their right, she could see the rectangular slab of a human box tomb rising above the ground. It wasn't much, but it was better than standing here in their bare paws.

"There!" she said, indicating with her nose. "If we can get on that, we might be safe. The scarabs don't seem to be climbing on anything—maybe they have to stay on the soil."

Biscuit gave her an agonised look. 'But that's too far! And there are scarabs on the ground between us! How are we going to reach it?"

"I can make it," said Ruffster. "Nothin' more than a Frisbee High Jump. But the smaller... ah, other dogs..." His eyes slid to Tyson.

"Leave that to me," said Honey. "You just get across first."

Ruffster gathered himself and started towards the box tomb. For a moment, it looked as if he would run straight into the mass of black beetles, but just as he reached the edge of the clear space, he launched himself with a mighty thrust of his haunches and leapt into the air. It was the same move Honey had seen him do a hundred times at the park when he jumped up to catch his Frisbee. They didn't call Ruffster the Canine Frisbee Champion for nothing. His body arched over the black swarm and landed lightly in the middle of the stone slab.

He looked back at them and wagged his

tail. "Piece o' liver cake!"

Biscuit started to follow, then whimpered and hovered uncertainly.

"C'mon, Biscuit!" yelled Ruffster, pacing back and forth on the box tomb. "You just got to take a runnin' jump!"

The Beagle took a deep breath and started running. His legs were shorter than Ruffster's and his podgy belly rolled from side to side as he ran. Honey held her breath as she watched him. *Would he make it?*

Biscuit launched himself into the air. He landed just on the edge of the tomb, his back paws scrabbling frantically to gain purchase on the smooth stone, then he rolled forwards and collapsed in the middle of the slab. They all breathed a sigh of relief.

Honey turned to Tyson. With his short, stubby legs, there was no way the Jack Russell could leap far enough to clear the space and land safely on the tomb. But if he was tossed, however... She reached for the scruff of his neck.

"No way!" the Jack Russell growled, backing away from her. "No dog is picking *me* up!"

"It's the only way," Honey pleaded. "You'll never make the leap by yourself! You're too—
"

"Small? Ya think I'm small, do ya?" snarled Tyson. "I'll show ya who's small!" He turned and started running towards the box tomb.

"No! Wait!" Honey started after him, horrified.

The Jack Russell leapt and for a moment, Honey thought he was going to make it. He was almost there, just a few inches short of the tomb. Then his paws flailed and his body plummeted like a stone, straight into the seething mass of black scarabs.

"Tyson!" Honey screamed, lunging forwards. But she was too far to reach him and all she managed to do was sling drool from her jowls in several directions. Frothy white slobber splattered the mass of black beetles around Tyson. There was a squelching sound. Several scarabs began staggering around, thrashing their legs against the slimy gloop that coated them. One scarab with drool on its head reeled backwards and crashed into several others, knocking them over and flipping them onto their backs where they rocked around, legs flailing.

"What?" Tyson scrambled to his feet and shook himself. He had landed with his teeth bared, ready to take on a killer beetle army, but instead he found himself surrounded by blobs of Dane slobber and helpless insect legs.

"Look!" Ruffster wagged his tail excitedly. They all followed his gaze.

The army of scarabs was breaking up as many beetles clumped together, struggling, in sticky blobs of drool. Others retreated, trying to avoid being slimed. Patches of open ground were appearing within the seething carpet of black bodies.

"Quick, Tyson—get out of there!" Honey said.

The Jack Russell leapt over some beetles to land in a clear patch of ground on his right. Then, using the other empty patches like stepping stones, he made his way to the path leading back to the cemetery gates. Biscuit hopped off the box tomb and followed Tyson's example, but Ruffster looked back at Honey, hesitating.

"I'm right behind you," said Honey. "Just go!"

Ruffster took off. Honey took a deep breath and looked around. While there was more clear ground near the tomb where the other dogs had been—around her the scarabs still seethed in a thick, black mass. The nearest patch of clear ground was several feet away. Honey whined and shuffled her paws. Danes might have some of the longest legs in the dog world, but they aren't good at leaping from standing. When you're built like a horse, you move like a horse too, and Honey knew that she needed space to get up into a full run before she could launch herself into a high jump. But now she barely had more than a few steps ahead of her.

Can I do it?

She had no choice. Already the scarabs were edging closer, the circle of space around her shrinking faster and faster. Honey looked towards the clear patch of ground again and gathered herself. She loped forwards a few steps, getting as close to the edge of the beetle army as she dared before pushing off with all her strength and launching herself into the air.

She landed just barely inside the patch of clear ground and her paws skimmed something hard and uneven. She stumbled; there was a crunch and a sharp prick of pain. She gulped and looked down. Nothing. Just some dry twigs under her paws. The scarabs were a few inches behind her. She had made it.

She darted across to the next patch of clear ground and then she was on the path. She started running. Ruffster was waiting for her just outside the cemetery gates. They glanced back. It was hard to see in the dark, but the scarabs didn't seem to be following.

"Where are the others?" Honey panted.

"They ran on ahead." Ruffster eyed her. "You OK, mate?"

Honey looked down at her right front paw where she had felt that prick of pain. She flexed her toes. Nothing. She put her weight down gingerly on her paw pad. Nothing. She sighed in relief and looked up at Ruffster. "Yes. I thought maybe... but it's nothing."

"C'mon, we'd better try to find the others." Ruffster turned and trotted off.

Honey followed him past Max's house with its high hedge and inscrutable front gate, back up Lemon Tree Lane. At the top of the lane, where it joined the bigger street leading back to the park, Ruffster paused to sniff a bush for any Peemail the others might have left them. He wagged his tail at Honey.

"I think they've gone this way!" He disappeared around the corner.

Honey started to follow, then froze in her

tracks, her eyes bulging.

On the pavement in front of her was a small, dark blur. A cat.

It was a very small cat—a tiny baby really—with its eyes barely open and its black fur just a smudge of fuzz around its little body. It must have just come out from under the bushes around the nearby house and now sat blinking in the glow of the street lights. The kitten turned as if sensing her and started wobbling in her direction.

CHAPTER 8

Honey backed quickly away from the kitten, her tail tucked under her belly.

"Hey, Honey, are you comin' or…" Ruffster poked his head back around the corner, then burst out laughing. "You're not doin' that stupid cat-phobia thing again?"

"It's not stupid," Honey mumbled, looking at the ground. "Cats are scary." She tried to edge her way around the kitten.

"Oh, for kibble's sake, Honey! It's barely the size o' your paw!" Ruffster trotted back towards her and the kitten. "I'll show you what to do!" He thrust his head out and charged at the kitten, barking at the top of his voice.

There was a tiny screech and hiss as the kitten puffed up to twice its size, then sprang for the nearest tree, scrambling to claw itself up to the lowest branches.

"That's the way to deal with cats," Ruffster said, grinning and giving himself a good shake. "Buddy the Lab says his technique is better—stalkin' and cornerin' them—but I don't think you can beat some good old-fashioned barkin' and chasin', myself."

Honey looked up at the tree uneasily. "Did you have to do that?"

"Hey, don't you start feelin' sorry for them! Cats always land on their feet—and get some poor mutt in trouble while they're at it." Ruffster sniffed in disgust and turned away. "C'mon." He disappeared around the corner again.

Honey slunk past the tree, trying not to look up, but she couldn't block her ears to the terrified mewling coming from the kitten. She hesitated and looked back. It was still clinging to the branch, trembling and crying, its eyes squeezed shut.

None of my business, Honey told herself firmly. It wasn't her fault the kitten had ended up in the tree. Anyway, she was sure some human would come along and rescue it soon. Or maybe the kitten would just climb back down on its own. Cats were great climbers, weren't they?

The kitten started trying to crawl back down the branch. Honey saw its tiny claws—still soft and transparent—slip and scrabble frantically at the bark, and her heart lurched as the kitten caught itself just in time. Honey moved towards the tree but stopped as the kitten's scent suddenly wafted over her. She recoiled. Although faint and milky, the Kitty Odour was unmistakable. She had never been this close to a cat before. Not even a tiny baby one.

She heard Ruffster's voice calling her and

she imagined him coming back and seeing what she was doing. *Helping a cat?* What was she thinking? She backed away from the tree. The kitten looked at her, trembling. Honey turned sharply and hurried around the corner, ignoring the pitiful cries behind her until they faded into the distance. She stopped, feeling sick and ashamed. *Not my business*, she told herself. *Not my business...*

She saw Ruffster further ahead and hurried to catch up with him. He was standing on the next street corner, checking Peemail on a lamp post. Honey watched absently, trying to put the image of the kitten out of her mind.

"Tyson left us a message," said Ruffster, looking up. "Warned us to be careful 'coz the Dog Catcher is doin' his rounds; he nearly caught them. They've gone home. Reckon we should do the same—gettin' late, you know. My Guy'll probably be gettin' worried about me."

"But..." Honey shook her head. "What about Bean and the other puppies?"

"Can't keep lookin' all night, can we? And what if the Dog Catcher gets us?"

Honey shuddered. Ruffster was right. She had no more leads to follow. What else could she do now but wander aimlessly around? Suddenly, she felt very, very tired. *First thing tomorrow morning*, she promised herself, *I'll start searching again*. She followed Ruffster as he led the way back towards the park and their homes.

The sound of ringing woke Honey from a fitful sleep the next morning. She raised her head blearily, drool clinging to her jowls, and furrowed her brow, trying to remember. Then it all came rushing back: Bean. The other puppies. Max. The cemetery. The scarabs. The kitten in the tree. She glanced out the window and was horrified to see how high the sun had climbed already. She had overslept.

She sprang out of bed and shook herself, then winced as a prick of pain stabbed her right front paw. She raised it and stared at it, her heart suddenly racing, but it looked normal. No bite marks, no swelling, no red sores. She licked it experimentally and put it back down on the ground, testing her weight. It felt normal. *You're turning into Suka*, she chided herself. It was probably just a scratch from one of those twigs in the cemetery. She gave her paw one more lick, then went into the kitchen

The Pet Sitter was at the kitchen table, surrounded by a jumble of papers. She was on the phone, talking fast, her voice high and anxious. Her eyes were red and her mouth wobbled as she talked. Honey looked at the papers on the table. They all had a picture of Bean with the words "Missing Puppy" written in large letters underneath, and more words and a number at the bottom.

The Pet Sitter put the phone down with a sigh and looked at Honey. "Where is she, Honey? Where is my puppy?"

Honey whined softly. The Pet Sitter patted

her head, then got up to give Honey her breakfast. Honey stared at the food in her bowl. She didn't feel hungry at all. But if she was going to spend all day searching for Bean, she couldn't afford to start out on an empty stomach.

She dipped her head and started eating while a part of her brain wondered how she could get out of the house. She had never tried escaping before—not like Biscuit and Suka, who both practically diplomas in C.E.E. (*Canine Escape Expertise*). They knew every loose panel in their fences and every rusty latch on their doors, whereas Honey had never even tried to put her head out the window.

But not today. Honey raised her head from the empty bowl and eyed the back door. Was there some way she could open it and then get out of the backyard without the Pet Sitter noticing?

A sound made her turn around. The Pet Sitter was standing by the kitchen table, the papers bunched up under one arm. In her other hand, she held out Honey's leash.

"Come on, Honey—we're going for a little walk so I can put up these posters."

Honey wagged her tail in delight. She wouldn't have to resort to escape to get out of the house after all!

Twenty minutes later, though, Honey was beginning to wonder if escaping would have been a better option. They had barely covered a few streets, what with the Pet Sitter stopping on every corner to stick a poster onto a lamp post, street bin, or bus stop. Honey paced around impatiently as they stopped yet again by another lamp post. Then her attention was caught by something across the street.

An old man was walking hurriedly past on the other side with a black dog trotting beside him. The morning sunlight passed over the rippling muscles and puckered scars on the dog's body. Max the Pit Bull. And Honey recognised the old man as the same man who had been in the kitchen last night. He was holding a bundle under one arm, his fingers clenched tight on the old towel around it as if struggling to keep it in place. Honey's heart flipped as she saw the bundle suddenly squirm and move.

She glanced back at the Pet Sitter, who was still intent on sticking a poster to the lamp post. The woman had dropped Honey's leash so that she could use both hands to wrap the poster better. Honey looked back to the other side of the street. Max and the Old Man were just disappearing from view around the corner. *What was in that bundle?*

Honey made her decision. Moving as quietly as she could, she crept across the street, dragging her leash behind her. Reaching the other side, she paused and glanced back. The Pet Sitter was still engrossed in her poster. Good. Honey hurried forwards to the street corner and peered around. She could see Max and the Old Man in the distance ahead. With one last glance at the Pet Sitter, Honey slipped around the corner and started to follow them.

CHAPTER 9

They were moving fast and seemed to be heading towards the centre of town. Honey followed as close as she dared but made sure she always stayed out of scenting distance. As long as she was downwind, she should be safe. The leash trailing behind her irritated her—she wished there was some way she could take it off—but at least it was nylon and made no noise other than a soft rasp on the concrete pavement as it dragged along.

Then she saw Max pause and turn his head, his nose twitching. She froze, wondering where she could hide if he should turn around. They were in a narrow street, surrounded on both sides by tall townhouses, and there wasn't even a bush for her to duck behind. But luck was with her: a terrier rushed out of the house ahead and threw himself against the fence, eyeballing Max and yelling insults at the top of his voice. The Old Man dragged Max away and after a moment, Honey resumed her steps behind them.

The street turned a corner and suddenly

they were in the town square. Honey had been here several times before with Olivia—the big, open space buzzed with activity as buses pulled up in one corner, their brakes hissing, while humans talked and laughed and banged their forks and spoons at the rickety café tables on the other. A million pigeons seemed to live in the square too, cooing and pecking their way between the benches or filling the sky with their fluttering wings.

Honey saw the Old Man pause and get a firmer grip on his bundle, then start briskly across the square, heading for the cluster of shops in the far corner. Max followed and after two beats, Honey slunk after them, dodging and weaving between the stream of people crossing the square. She saw a few of them stare at her in surprise and hoped that none of them would be curious enough to stop and find out why she was wandering loose on her own. That was the problem with being a dog the size of a pony—you could never get away with sneaking anywhere unnoticed, unlike some of her other dog friends.

One man who was walking past paused, took out his iBone, and pointed it at Honey. She stiffened, hunching her shoulders and lowering her head while averting her eyes. A small white light flashed. The man grinned, then slipped the iBone back in his pocket and hurried away. Honey breathed a sigh of relief. It was Morning Time, she remembered—people were probably too busy thinking about going to their Jobs or Schools or other human things to bother with a dog. Besides, her trailing leash might make people think her human was nearby.

She remembered Max and the Old Man and jerked her head around just in time to see them disappear into a shop on the far corner of the square. Ignoring the looks from bystanders, Honey bounded after them and pulled up in front of the store. It was the old pet shop.

Maybe she'd been wrong? Maybe Max and his Old Man were just on an innocent trip to get some kibble and chews? Honey peered in through the big glass windows, trying to see past the cages filled with straw and the bags of kibble stacked high. She saw the Old Man, but he wasn't looking at anything on the shelves. Instead, he was heading straight for a door at the back of the shop. He disappeared into the back room, still clutching his bundle, and she saw Max's tail whisk after him.

Honey whined in frustration. *Where was he taking that bundle? What was he doing with it?* She looked doubtfully at the open doorway of the pet shop. Could she just walk in and hope that the guy at the counter would ignore her like the humans outside in the square had done?

A soft voice said over her shoulder, "What is the matter?"

Honey whirled around. It was the new dog she'd met in the park yesterday, the one called Newbie. He was standing behind her, looking at her quizzically.

"Oh..." Honey stammered "Um... I was just... you know, waiting..."

Newbie nodded. "Yesss. I also. My new family are at the butcher..." He waved his nose at a door a few shops down. "Perhapsss they will get me a bone... Do you like bones?"

"Uh... yeah... sure," Honey said, her eyes straying back to the pet-shop window. Nobody had come out of the back room yet. She scanned the rest of the shop just to be sure. Aside from the young guy at the counter, it seemed to be empty. There was some movement from a few cages in the corner—a rabbit reared itself up, twitching its whiskers, while a bird flapped its wings in another cage overhead—but Honey couldn't see any other person or dog in the store.

No, wait.... In the corner of the shop was a puppy pen. Honey peered closely. There, amongst the newspapers and squeaky toys, she could see the shape of a skinny puppy curled up on his side. He must have been in the pet shop for a while already; he looked about four months old and no longer had that soft puppy roundness. His head seemed too big for his body, hanging on the end of a scrawny neck, and his legs were short and stubby. He was black with a scruffy coat and little whiskers on his chin that would probably morph into a shaggy beard when he was fully grown.

Newbie stepped up beside her and followed her gaze. "It is very sad... to be unwanted like that."

"Unwanted?" Honey looked at him in

surprise.

"He is not fortunate, that puppy," said Newbie, his eyes on the sleeping pup. "He does not have the fluffy, white fur and big, floppy ears that humans always like…. He is different, and therefore ugly and ignored. They are shallow, humans—they choose with their eyes, not with their hearts."

Honey looked back at the puppy, feeling slightly embarrassed. She knew she had been lucky to be born into the home of a Responsible Breeder, cherished and loved, with a family carefully selected for her and a human who had waited a long time to have her. But many other dogs were not so fortunate. They were born to sickly mothers in the dreaded Puppy Farms and languished in small, cramped cages in pet stores, only to be bought on impulse and sometimes abandoned again when the fickle humans tired of them. She looked at Newbie—at the way his mouth twisted as if tasting a bitter heartworm pill—and wondered if he had been a pet store puppy once himself. But she didn't dare ask.

"Um… so, how… how are you settling in?" she said.

"It is a nice town," Newbie said. "I have much to do."

"That's a beautiful collar," said Honey, eyeing the gold band around his neck. It was studded with large blue stones the colour of the sky, and it had an oval disc dangling from the middle. She could see something etched on the disc and guessed that it must be some kind of fancy name tag. "Your new family must really spoil you."

"Yesss, they do," said Newbie. "But this is not from them. It is from my passst life."

"Oh." Honey felt curiosity eating at her again but still she hesitated. She knew Ruffster would probably have just barged in and asked him, and Suka would have wormed his entire history out of him by now, but Honey hated being pushy. Still, maybe he was just shy; maybe he would love to tell her more about himself.

She opened her mouth, then shifted suddenly, aware for the first time of a dull throbbing in her right front paw. *When had that started?* She stared down at it. In the centre of her right paw, just by the knuckles of her toes, a small bump was now visible. Honey blinked. It must have been a trick of the morning light, but for a moment, she thought the bump had moved under her skin. She looked up to see Newbie watching her with his pale yellow eyes.

"Is something wrong?"

Honey swallowed. "N...no, nothing."

A voice calling Newbie's name made them both turn around. A man and woman were standing outside the butcher's shop, patting their knees and calling to him.

"I mussst go," said Newbie. He glanced at her paw again, then turned and trotted off.

Honey stared after him, half-relieved to see him go. She looked back down at her paw. She was sure the throbbing had lessened now. Maybe she'd sprained her paw running across the square. She turned back to the pet-shop window, trying not to think about her paw, and scanned the interior of the shop again. Still no sign of Max and his Old Man. *What were they doing in that back room?*

The sound of footsteps made her turn around. A man was walking briskly towards the pet shop. Honey glanced back into the store, then at the approaching man, and an idea crossed her mind. Just as the man passed her, she fell into step behind him and followed him into the pet shop, looking up at him attentively as if he were her master. The guy at the counter glanced up as they entered, then looked away. Honey wagged her tail in elation. It had worked.

There was a metal display wall down the middle of the shop with collars and leashes hanging on one side and dog and cat toys hanging on the other. Honey ducked behind this and used it to block her from view as she made her way to the back of the store. She paused outside the doorway to the back room, sniffing the air. It gave her just enough warning to jump back and duck behind a tall aquarium as Max and his Old Man suddenly emerged from the back room. Honey peeked around the side of the aquarium. The Old Man's hands were empty.

She watched them leave the shop, then turned her attention back to the doorway. She sniffed the air again, then stepped cautiously through into the back room.

It took a moment for her eyes to become accustomed to the dim light. The back room was much bigger than she had expected—it seemed to be a large garage that was being used as a storeroom. Bags of dry dog food were piled along one wall next to bales of straw and sacks of bird seed. Another wall had shelves crammed with an assortment of cat and dog collars, leashes, and grooming brushes. Honey caught her breath as she saw something on the worktable next to the shelves. An old, discarded towel. The same towel she had seen wrapped around the bundle the old man had been holding.

She looked frantically around the rest of the room. On the far side, next to a pile of dog beds, was a large garage door. It was rolled up and open, showing the alleyway outside the back of the pet shop. A white van was parked there and Honey saw a man standing beside the open van door. He was holding something in his arms, but his back was to her and she couldn't see what it was. She heard voices and the man cursing as he struggled with whatever was in his arms. Then he stepped back and slammed the door shut. The van engine roared to life.

The man waved, then returned to the storeroom, pulling the roller door down behind him. It slid down with a loud clacking noise and was almost fully closed when the man looked up and spotted Honey. His eyes widened.

Honey backed quickly out of the room and turned, almost crashing into the tall aquarium. The guy at the counter looked up and shouted, but Honey ignored him as she tore through the shop, back towards the square outside. She had to find out where that white van was going.

"*Hey! What the—?*"

Her trailing leash caught on the side of a shelf and jerked her to a stop. Honey threw a desperate look behind her, then lunged forwards. The leash snapped free, yanking the whole shelf unit sideways and causing boxes and bottles to tumble to the ground behind her.

More shouting.

Honey raced out of the pet shop, swerved onto the street, and darted down the narrow side lane beside the shop, finally emerging in the back alleyway just in time to see the white van gliding smoothly away.

CHAPTER 10

Honey galloped as fast as she could, straining to keep the white van in sight. Her leash flapped along behind her and she hoped fervently that it wouldn't get caught on anything else. The van slowed down as it turned a corner, and for a moment, Honey thought she could close the distance between them—but she could no longer ignore the throbbing in her front paw. The pain was making her wince with each step. She rounded the corner after the van and stumbled, nearly falling over. The van revved its engine, then sped up again, and she saw it rumble down the road, which joined the Big Highway that took you out of town.

Honey stopped and panted heavily, drool hanging from her jowls in thick strings. She watched the van disappear from sight, her ears down and tail drooping. She had lost it.

Had Bean and the other puppies been inside that van? Had she lost her chance to find them? Hanging her head, Honey turned around and started walking back the way she had come. At the end of the street, she paused and sat down to lick her front right paw. Her pad was raw and tender from the hard running, but that wasn't where the throbbing was coming from. It was coming from the lump. She stared at it. It had grown bigger.

No. She was imagining things.

She forced her eyes away and stood up, giving herself a good shake. Then she looked around with new interest. She realised where she was: just around the corner from Lemon Tree Lane. She thought of the kitten in the tree again. *None of my business*, Honey reminded herself, and yet somehow her legs started moving, taking her back towards the tree. She halted a few feet from it and squinted up into the branches. *Surely it must have been rescued by now?*

Then she saw it. That pale smudge of black fur. It was still clinging to the lowest branch, but now the kitten looked limp and weak, its little body barely moving. It turned its head as it heard her and let out a feeble mew.

Honey felt sick with guilt and shame. The kitten had been left up in the tree all night—cold, scared, and hungry—and now it was weak, maybe even dying. She should have rescued it yesterday. She should have done something.

But it wasn't too late to do the right thing.

Honey took a determined breath. She stepped closer to the tree and felt the old cat phobia grip her as the scent of the kitten filled her nostrils. Drool pooled in her jowls. All her senses were screaming *CAT! RUN!* but she fought down the panic and forced herself to look up instead. The kitten was wedged right where the lowest branch joined the main trunk, which was still fairly high up, but the one good thing about being a Great Dane is that there isn't much you can't reach.

Honey heaved herself up until she was standing on her hind legs. She braced her front paws on the tree trunk and grabbed the kitten gently by its scruff. It wriggled wildly for a moment, then went limp. She lowered it carefully to the ground and opened her jaws. The kitten rolled out and lay there, wet with slobber and rigid with shock. Then its mouth opened and Honey saw the pink inside as it made a little gasping noise.

"Meowmy! Meowmy!" Its tiny paws paddled the air.

Honey stared at it, wondering what to do. She didn't know much about babies, but she knew this little one was cold and weak. She needed to do something. Then a memory stirred. When she was a baby herself, she had wriggled away from the warm pile of her brothers and sisters. Suddenly, she had been alone: blind, lost, and scared. And she had opened her mouth and cried, just like this kitten was doing now. Then her mother's head had been there and a warm tongue and a wonderful *rubbing, rubbing, rubbing* all over her body.

Honey bent her head. She knew what she

had to do. Tentatively, she licked the kitten, then slowly with firmer and firmer strokes as the trembling in the tiny body slowed and finally changed into a rhythmic vibration. *Purring.* The kitten was purring!

Honey nosed the kitten gently, rolling it over and sniffing it carefully for any signs of injury. It seemed OK. But she smelled something else that made her stiffen. A strong feline scent. The kitten's mother, she realised. And she also realised where she had smelled the same scent before. Last night, in the back alley behind Max's house, when Biscuit had disturbed that black feral cat near the bins... that must have been the kitten's mother, searching for food.

Honey thought of Biscuit's narrow escape from those ferocious claws and cringed. But she knew she had no choice. The kitten was weak and hungry and would die if it didn't get its mother's milk soon. She picked it up again by the scruff of its neck. It relaxed and dangled happily from her mouth as she started making her way down Lemon Tree Lane.

As she neared the high hedge around Max's house, Honey kept a wary eye on the open gates of the cemetery beyond. But all seemed quiet today. No sinister *click-clicking*, no scuttling black bodies, no scarabs. Carrying the kitten carefully, she stepped into the narrow passageway and hurried through to the back alley behind Max's house.

The bins were still there and Honey could smell the fresh rubbish inside, the rank scent even stronger this morning. She approached the bins hesitantly, her eyes searching the shadows behind them. *Would the feral cat still be there?*

A sudden hiss made her jump backwards and almost drop the kitten. A black shape detached itself from the shadows and prowled towards her. The morning light showed the fur to be dark tortoiseshell rather than black, but the cat's eyes were just as fierce as last night. She hissed at Honey again, and the strong tang of Kitty Odour wafted across. Honey began trembling. She lowered her head, carefully depositing the kitten on the ground in front of her, and backed away.

The feral cat came forwards and sniffed the kitten, her whiskers curling back in disgust as she smelled Honey's drool on the kitten's fur. Then the kitten let out a faint mew and its mother softened. A faint rumbling filled the air as the feral cat began purring and washing the kitten. Honey watched, mesmerised, as the pink tongue rasped again and again over the kitten's fur before the feral cat finally seemed satisfied. She picked the kitten up in her mouth and turned to go—then paused and swung her fierce eyes back to Honey.

Honey dropped her ears and lowered her head, averting her eyes, and gave her tail a hesitant wag. The feral cat looked at Honey for a long moment, then a soft meow issued from her throat. Honey looked up in surprise. The feral cat blinked twice in affection and thanks, and then she was gone, taking the kitten with her.

"That kitten was lucky."

Honey whirled around. Max the Pit Bull was standing behind her.

CHAPTER 11

Max stood beside the high hedge, a few feet behind her. She wondered how long he had been there. She scanned the back of his property, trying to see how he had got out.

"I found the hole that you and your friends made last night," he said, as if reading her thoughts.

"I...I saw you this morning," Honey blurted out. "With your Old Man. He was carrying something."

Max said nothing, his eyes watchful.

"What was in the bundle?" Honey asked.

"It's nothing to do with you."

Honey felt anger surge into her chest. "How can you say it's nothing to do with me? Was it a puppy? Is your Old Man stealing puppies?" She stopped suddenly, realizing she was snapping and snarling in Max's face. She pulled back and said bitterly, "I thought you were different... but my friends were right about you. They said you can't trust a Pit Bull—you're just a liar and a psycho!"

Max stiffened. Then he said quietly, "I give

you my word—that bundle is nothing to do with the missing puppies."

Honey stared at him, then turned and stalked past him towards the narrow passageway.

Max stepped into her path and looked at her sharply. "You're hurt."

Honey tried to hide her surprise. "W...why do you say that?" She stood up straighter, ignoring the throbbing pain in her front paw. "There's nothing wrong with me."

Max narrowed his eyes. "I know about weakness and pain... to size up another dog and find his vulnerabilities. That's what I was trained for, what made the difference between life and death in the pit." He paused, then said quietly, "You're hurt somewhere."

"I... I'm fine," said Honey.

"The pain... it's getting worse, isn't it?"

Honey didn't reply, but whatever he saw in her eyes must have given him an answer.

"Wait here." Max ducked under the hedge and wriggled through the hole leading back into his garden. A moment later he returned, his jaws crammed with a bunch of pale green leaves. He dropped these on the ground in front of him.

"*Cacahuatl* leaves. They grow in my garden. They'll help with the pain."

His voice was gentle and Honey felt ashamed of her earlier outburst. Suddenly she wanted to trust Max. She walked over, lowered her head, and sniffed the leaves. They had a strong odour, a bit similar to the dried tea leaves that Olivia kept in a jar in the kitchen, but otherwise they looked pretty ordinary. She hesitated, glanced up at Max, then took a few in her mouth and chewed slowly. Bitterness at first, then a warming numbness filled her mouth. The warmth continued to spread down her throat and throughout her body. She took another mouthful and chewed some more, breathing deeply. The throbbing in her front paw faded slightly, the pain dulled and receded.

Honey gave a grateful wag of her tail and reached down again to eat some more—then froze as she suddenly focused on Max's paws next to the pile of leaves. The right paw had the normal four toes, but the left paw had a toe missing, leaving just three toes. *Three toes.* Honey remembered those paw prints in the cemetery and jerked backwards.

"What is it?" Max looked at her in surprise.

Disappointment flooded her, tasting more bitter than the *cacahuatl* leaves had in her mouth. She had believed him, trusted him! But he had lied to her. He must have been in the cemetery with the puppies. He must have been the one who made those strange paw prints amongst the puppy tracks, the prints with only three toes.

"Honey?"

"I have to go," Honey said, backing away. She turned, tail between her legs, and dived into the narrow passageway, ignoring Max's voice behind her. She felt stupid and betrayed. How could she have thought she could trust him?

Emerging back into Lemon Tree Lane, she quickened her steps, wanting to get as far away as possible. She swerved at the top of the lane where it joined the bigger street and started running, not sure where she was going but just needing to get away. She rounded a corner and collided with a furry body.

"Howling hyenas, Honey! What's the hurry?"

It was Suka the Siberian Husky. She stared at Honey, bright-eyed, her fluffy tail waving. Behind her, red-faced and puffing, came a woman being towed on the end of the leash. Honey recognised her as the Boy's Mother who used to chat with Olivia in the park sometimes. She was nice, although she had a scary voice when she was shouting at Suka. Her face brightened now as she saw Honey and she came up, smiling and reaching out to pat Honey on the head. Then she picked up Honey's trailing leash and looked around, frowning. As if reaching a decision, she looped the leash through her hand and started walking back the way she had come, giving Honey a gentle tug to bring her along.

Honey fell into step beside Suka, who was once more pulling in front. The Husky looked at Honey expectantly.

"What happened last night, Honey? Did you find your pup? I tried to follow you dogs, but my Boy's Mother caught me and dragged me home."

Honey quickly filled Suka in on what

happened last night at Max's house and the cemetery, plus this morning at the pet store, although she didn't mention the pain in her paw nor what had just happened in the alley behind Max's house.

Suka's blue eyes opened wide. "The pet shop! That's where those other puppies were stolen from too! So that bundle... do you think it was a puppy?"

Honey hesitated. "I...I don't know."

"I'll bet it was! I'll bet the Old Man is involved in some puppy-kidnapping ring! Maybe he steals them and gives them to the dogfighting gangs. And Max is totally helping him, don't you think?"

Honey thought of the three-toed paw print in the cemetery and shifted uncomfortably.

"What about the cemetery?" asked Suka. "Did you find any other clues there?"

"Well, we were sort of tied up with those scarabs, you know," Honey said dryly. "That one memorial stone, though... it was so strange. It had a really weird name carved on it and some other words—"

"What did the words say?"

"I don't remember exactly," Honey admitted. "Something about a curse if you disturb things." Honey shut her eyes, trying to remember. "*He who disturbs... awaken the curse...* Oh, and then something about black hunger. *Black hunger on skin, consume from within.* That's it."

The words reminded Honey of the lump on her front paw, stirring under her skin. She pushed the thought away and said hurriedly,

"It wasn't just words... there were some pictures too. But not like the pictures on the other marker stones. These were creepy."

"Like what?"

Honey furrowed her brow. "There were eyes... and human hands and feet... and some birds with hooked beaks... and funny zigzags and squiggles—"

"Wait!' Suka exclaimed, her eyes suddenly round. "I think I know where those pictures come from! I think I might know what they mean!"

CHAPTER 12

If Suka had been pulling before, it was nothing compared to the way she was ploughing down the path now, so impatient was she to get back to her house and show Honey what she was talking about.

"You'll see what I mean! In my Boy's books! I was just looking at them yesterday, when I was helping him with his homework!" Suka panted, straining against her harness.

Honey trotted to keep up with her and glanced back at the Boy's Mother, who was being hauled along, jogging and tripping behind them, her arms taut with the effort of holding on to Suka's leash.

"Er... shouldn't you slow down a bit?" Honey suggested. "My human's really strict about me not pulling on the leash."

Suka shrugged. "Well, if she doesn't want me to pull, she shouldn't put a harness on me, should she? I'm a Husky. I pull. That's what I do."

They rounded a corner and the Boy's Mother sighed in relief as they arrived in front of Suka's house. She glared at Suka and massaged her arms as she fished in her pockets for the key. But before she could unlock the front door, they heard a shout from the street.

They all turned to look. It was Biscuit on a leash, walking with his Missus, who was smiling and waving now as she approached the garden gate. The Boy's Mother smiled and called back.

"Come in! I've just got back from our walk; I was going to put the kettle on. Want a cuppa? And look who I found wandering near the cemetery! Poor dog—she looks like she's been running around for hours. I thought Olivia said she'd gotten a pet sitter to come look after Honey? I must ring her house when we get in and tell the girl I've got Honey here. Anyway, come in! Come in! I've got a couple of hours before I need to pick Tommy up from school."

They followed her inside and the dogs waited impatiently for the humans to unclip their leashes. The two women headed into the kitchen, leaving them alone in the hallway.

"You got anything to eat?" Biscuit looked mournfully at Suka. "My Missus only gave me half rations this morning."

"Come up to my Boy's room," said Suka. "There's always some food in there. I know he had some cookies last night. Anyway, I've got to show Honey something." She turned and led the way up the stairs, taking them two at a time. Honey went up more carefully—stairs can be a bit tricky when you've got long Great

Dane legs—and Biscuit brought up the rear, huffing and puffing behind them.

"Maybe your humans are right about a diet," said Suka, eyeing Biscuit as he heaved himself, panting, over the top step. "You look like you could totally lose some weight."

"Me?" Biscuit said indignantly. "I'm not fat!"

"What d'you call that?" said Suka, poking his podgy belly with her paw.

"That's... that's just the way us Beagles look," said Biscuit with a haughty sniff. "We're a nice, solid breed, not like some of those weedy, scrawny dogs. Anyway, where are those cookies?"

Suka rolled her eyes. "This way."

She led them into a room at the end of the landing. Honey and Biscuit hovered in the doorway and wondered how to go in, for the floor was so littered with things that there was hardly space to put a paw: books and papers and bags with smelly socks falling out; little human figures and plastic cars, pencils, and footballs; and lots of those shiny music discs everywhere.

Suka leapt nimbly over a chessboard and climbed onto the Boy's bed, pushing the rumpled blankets aside. Biscuit started to follow, then stopped, his nose twitching. He unearthed a plate half-hidden under a stack of magazines, its surface still smeared with breadcrumbs and marmalade. Honey left him licking the plate ecstatically as she stepped carefully over the mess on the floor to reach the bed. She tried to climb on too, but the space next to Suka was taken up by a big wooden thing with a stick pointing out one end and lots of strings stretched across it.

"Careful!" Suka said. "That's my Boy's guitar! Maybe you'd better stay off the bed. Anyway, the thing I wanted to show you is here; you're tall enough to see it standing up." She put her paws onto the Boy's desk, next to the bed, and nosed among the pile of books there. "Here it is!"

Suka pulled out one thick book and flipped the pages with her paws, pausing finally at a page with a chart taking up half the space. In the chart were rows upon rows of little pictures. Honey stepped closer to the desk and looked—then did a double take. Suka was right. These were just like the pictures on the strange memorial stone!

A: 🦅 B: 🦵 C: 🍞 D: 🐍 E: 🦶 F: 🐦
G: 🏺 H: 𓎝 I: 🦚 J: 🐍 K: 🥣 L: 🦁 M: 🦅
N: 〰 O: 🦅 P: □ Q: △ R: 👄 S: 🪶 T: 🍞
U: 𓃹 V: 🐍 W: 🐤 X: ⊖ Y: 𓏭 Z: ⚋

"What are these?" Honey asked excitedly.

"They're pictures made by the humans in Old Egypt," said Suka. "My Boy's been learning about them. They have a special name... *hypo... hydro...* No, *hieroglyphics*; that's it, yeah. *Hieroglyphics.*" Suka looked hopefully at Honey. "So are they the ones?"

"Yes," said Honey, her eyes roving over the little pictures. "Yes, they're just like the pictures on that memorial stone!"

"Which ones? Can you remember?"

Honey furrowed her brow and leaned closer, thinking hard. The throbbing had started in her front paw again, which made it hard to concentrate. After Max had given her those leaves, the pain had faded, but now it seemed to be coming back. She wriggled her toes and glanced down surreptitiously: the lump was still there. In fact, it had definitely moved. It was further up now, by the big knuckle above her paw, and the skin over it was stretched taut. She tore her eyes away and looked back at the book, trying to focus on the pictures.

Suka peered at Honey. "Are you all right? You look a bit... funny."

"Yeah, I'm fine," said Honey quickly, shifting her weight so that she was standing less on the throbbing front paw.

Biscuit jumped up on the bed next to Suka, licking his chops. There were breadcrumbs still stuck to his nose. "What's going on? What am I missing?"

"These pictures... Honey says they're like the ones on that strange memorial stone in the cemetery!" Suka looked at Biscuit. "What does the famous Beagle nose say?"

Biscuit gave a serious nod and climbed onto the desk. He stuck his nose into the book, inhaling deeply in the centre crease between the pages. "Mm... there're some cookie crumbs stuck down here. What flavour cookies did you say your Boy was eating last night?"

"Biscuit!"

"OK, OK..." The Beagle sat back on his haunches. "Yeah, they're the same as the ones in the cemetery, but I don't know why you're getting so excited over a bunch of stupid pictures anyway."

"Because my Boy says that they're more than just pictures—they're a kind of writing too."

"Writing?"

"Yes! See the letters under each picture? Well, it's like a code. So if you match up the pictures to the letters, you can spell out the words. See?" Suka pushed the book back towards Honey. "Do you remember the order of any of the pictures?"

Honey thought hard. "Yes, there was one set that kept repeating—it was the leaf followed by the zigzag line, then a box, then that bird with the stubby wings."

"So what does that say?" asked Biscuit.

Suka pored over the chart, matching the letters with the pictures. "*Inpw.*"

"Huh?"

"What does *that* mean?"

"I don't know." Suka shrugged, disappointed. "I thought it was going to give us some great clue to the puppies."

"Never mind." Honey's ears drooped. She

turned away from the book, discouraged as well. "Maybe the best place to look for clues is back at the pet shop. You said that's where some of the other puppies disappeared. I saw a puppy in there; maybe he saw something that night and can give us a lead."

"I'm coming with you this time," said Suka, jumping off the bed and following Honey to the door. "I'm not missing out on all the excitement!"

"The only thing is, how are we going to get back there?" said Honey "Your Boy's Mother was going to call my Pet Sitter and she'll take me back home."

"Oh, that's easy!" laughed Suka. "You've obviously never done the Dawn Breakout. That's the best time for escaping. You get up really early—like just before dawn—and hassle the humans to take you out to do your business. They'll be really sleepy at that time and won't be paying much attention to what you're doing. Once you're out of the house, you just slip away. By the time they realise you're gone, it'll be too late!"

"But... what about gates and fences?" asked Honey. "I still have to get out of my garden."

"Oh, there are always gaps and holes if you look hard enough. A lot of the time they don't shut the front gate properly and some houses don't have gates or fences anyway. Trust me! I've done it loads of times!" Suka wagged her tail. "Ask Biscuit—he's an expert at the Dawn Breakout too."

Suka looked back towards the Beagle who

was still sitting on the Boy's desk, his head down amongst the books. In fact, he seemed to be eating something and they both heard the sound of ripping paper.

"Biscuit!" Suka gasped "What are you doing?" She sprang back across the room and stared, horrified. "You've been eating my Boy's book!"

"Sorry!" Biscuit scrambled off the desk and gave a sheepish wag of his tail. "I was trying to get those cookie crumbs, although the page didn't taste bad either." He winced at Suka's glare. "I mean, sorry! It was an accident!"

Suka growled, her hackles bristling, and for a moment, Honey thought she was going to launch herself at Biscuit. When it came to her Boy, Suka could be ferocious. Everybody knew about the time she chased some of the school bullies halfway across town because they had pushed her Boy and made him cry.

Then they heard voices on the landing and the humans appeared at the top of the stairs.

"Suka! What are you doing?" the Boy's Mother demanded, coming into the room.

Suka glared at Biscuit, then turned and stalked away. Biscuit scurried over to his Missus, huddling by her legs.

The Boy's Mother clapped her hands. "Come on, pups, time to break up the party. Honey, your pet sitter is waiting for you downstairs." She shooed them towards the stairs.

Honey turned hurriedly to Suka. "I'll try your idea. Tomorrow morning. Before dawn. Can you get a Peemail to the others—

Ruffster and Tyson? They might like to come too."

Suka glowered at Biscuit, who was hurrying down the stairs ahead of them, then nodded. "All right, I'll tell them. Where shall we meet?"

"At the pet shop."

CHAPTER 13

The sun was still barely more than a streak of pale orange on the horizon when Honey arrived at the town square the next morning. It was strange how silent and deserted it was. The pigeons were just black specks clustered together on the roof of the buildings, and the shops and cafés were mostly still closed, although Honey could see a few doors open and a few people moving around, arranging tables and chairs on the pavement.

She paused to rest, shifting her weight off her right front paw. The pain had lessened in the night, but a cold numbness had begun spreading through her paw and up her leg, and this scared her more. She glanced down. The lump had definitely moved up her leg now, protruding just above her knuckle, and the numbness seemed to be spreading with it. *Will it keep invading my body?*

Honey yanked her thoughts away and focused on this morning instead, wondering if the other dogs had managed to get out.

Escaping had been much easier than she had expected. Suka had been right—the Pet Sitter had tottered obediently out when Honey had woken her up and asked to go out the front door. She had followed Honey out into the front garden, yawning and rubbing her eyes, and had barely paid attention as Honey crept across the lawn and pushed her way out of the unlatched front gate. Honey hadn't even heard a cry behind her as she loped away down the street.

Oh, she was sure there would be a hunt for her soon; they might even call the Dog Catcher this time. But it was still early now, with the world barely awake. Honey thought she had at least a few hours.

She started across the square, trying not to limp. As she approached the pet shop, she could see a huddle of shapes outside: Tyson waiting grimly, Biscuit sitting as far away as possible from Suka who was pacing up and down in front of the shop. Ruffster was giving himself a vigorous scratch, but he jumped up when he saw Honey and ran over to meet her, his one upright ear cocked in excitement.

"Thought you'd never get here, Honey!" He ran around her and sniffed her bum in greeting. "You figured out how we're goin' to get in?"

"There's a way in at the back, I think." Honey stumbled and winced, taking the weight off her right front paw.

"Hey, you all right, mate?" Ruffster paused and looked at her. "Hurt your leg or somethin'?"

"It's nothing," said Honey quickly. "Come on."

The others followed her as she led the way around the side of the pet shop to the alleyway at the back. The roller door was down, but Honey thought she could see a gap along the bottom. She remembered how it had not slid completely shut when the man had seen her yesterday. Maybe in all the excitement he had forgotten to go back and fix the door.

She went forwards eagerly. Yes, there was definitely a gap along the bottom—big enough for her to push her nose under. She turned back to the others, thinking she could ask Tyson to squeeze through first, but before she could say anything, Ruffster had shoved his head into the gap to look inside.

"Holy liver treat, Honey, check this out!" Ruffster said. "They keep all the good stuff back here! Look at those chew bones... and that tug toy... and those whopper dog biscuits—"

"Dog biscuits? Where?" Biscuit pushed Honey out of the way as he tried to look in the opening as well. His nose quivered, taking in all the scents from the room inside. "Oh my Dog! I can smell liver cookies! And those peanut-butter crackers with the carob sprinkles! Quick! I've got to get in there!"

Before anyone could stop him, Biscuit shoved his body into the gap, wriggling and pushing. The roller door creaked and groaned, then with a loud *clack-clack-clack*, it shot up several inches as Biscuit heaved himself through. There was a wide gap now. Ruffster dived in after Biscuit, followed by Tyson. Honey and Suka ducked under and crawled through on their bellies.

Honey stood up slowly and looked around. The room looked exactly like yesterday, except that the towel from the bundle was no longer on the worktable. A few feet from them, a bag of kibble had fallen off the pile and split open. Biscuit gave a bark of delight and pounced on the bag. In less than a minute, the bag was empty. Biscuit gave a burp and a metallic voice floated out from his stomach: "*You have no more messages.*"

"Mate, you're not normal," said Ruffster, staring in awe.

"Yeah, what normal dog would eat a book?" said Suka, glaring.

"Come on," said Honey, leading the way out of the storeroom. "We haven't got much time."

They stepped into the main store and paused as their eyes adjusted to the gloom. A few wooden hutches lined one wall, and through the mesh, they could see long, floppy ears and furry bodies. Next to the hutches were several cages filled with shredded tissue and plastic tunnels—from the high-pitched squeaks, Honey guessed there were mice inside. Across from the hutches was a row of shelves with dog and cat toys and in the far corner was the puppy pen.

A little black shape rushed to the side of the pen and sprang up on his hind legs. His too-big head bobbed on his scrawny neck and his tail wagged like crazy as he bounced in a way that reminded Honey of Bean.

"Who're you?"

"I'm Honey." She walked over to touch noses with the puppy. "What's your name?"

"I haven't got one," said the black puppy sadly. "Nobody's adopted me and given me a name yet. The people in the shop call me 'Here, Pup-pup' sometimes."

"I got called that too when I was a baby." Honey licked his nose. "Were you here when those other puppies disappeared?"

The black puppy shrank back a little. "Yes."

"You saw what happened, mate?" asked Ruffster, hurrying forwards. The others followed him and crowded around the puppy pen. The black puppy stared at them, his eyes wide. He had never seen so many different dogs before. He looked from Suka to Biscuit to Tyson to Honey and cowered back from them.

"Don't be frightened," said Honey. "We won't hurt you. We're just trying to find out what happened to the other puppies. Can you tell us what you saw that night?"

"I...I don't know." The black puppy pawed his eyes. "I was sleeping I think, and then I heard a noise... Like... like a clicking...?"

"Clicking? Oh, the scarabs!" said Biscuit.

"S...scarabs?" The puppy looked at them, his eyes filled with fear.

"They're like these ugly black beetles, mate," said Ruffster.

"Oh!" The puppy turned to stare at

something in the corner of his pen. "Th...there's one there."

Honey reached her neck over the side of the pen to nose amongst the blankets. She lifted out a dead scarab in her mouth and dropped it on the floor outside the pen. In the faint light that came in through the pet-store windows, the black shell gleamed dully.

Ruffster gave it a wary sniff. "Yeah, same as the ones that were found when the other pups went missin'."

Honey peered at the scarab more closely. There were marks etched on its black shell, she realised. And her heart began beating faster as she recognised what they were. The same pictures she'd remembered seeing on that memorial stone in the cemetery. The leaf, the zigzag line, the box, and the bird with stubby wings. The pictures that spelled out "*Inpw*".

"What happened after you heard the clicking?" Honey turned back to the puppy.

"I looked around for the other puppies but the pen was empty, except for me."

"How come ya didn't get taken?" growled Tyson.

"Nobody ever wants me," said the black puppy in a small voice.

"Hey, mate, don't be sad," said Ruffster, licking the top of the puppy's head. "Trust me, this is one party you don't want to get invited to."

The black puppy looked down at his paws again. "He said I was too old."

"Who?"

"The scary dog."

Honey inhaled sharply as she suddenly heard Bean's voice in her head again. *"Doggie scary"* she had said as they had walked away from Max.

"What scary dog?" asked Suka. "There was another dog here?"

The black puppy nodded. "He asked me how old I was, and when I told him I was sixteen weeks, he said I was too old."

"Too old for what?" said Ruffster, puzzled.

The puppy hunched miserably. "It's like when humans come to the store. They always look at the younger puppies and choose them. Nobody ever looks at me. Maybe I'm an ugly puppy." His head sank down to his paws. "I've been here for months now. I'm never going to find a Forever Home."

Honey didn't know what to say. She wanted to make the puppy feel better, but she thought back to Newbie's words outside the pet shop yesterday and cringed. It was a cruel, cruel thing keeping a puppy in a pet store, cooped up in a cage. Honey wondered if he had ever seen the sun or played outside in the fresh air.

"You're not an ugly puppy." Honey gave the puppy a lick. "You mustn't think that."

"Hey, don't give up, mate," Ruffster said to the puppy. "Me and my brothers were dumped on the street and we got taken to the rescue shelter. That's where all the really kind humans go lookin' for their dogs... and I was waitin' and waitin' for months. Nobody wanted me 'coz I was just this scruffy mutt with ears that didn't even match up, and then one day my Guy walked in and we looked at each other... And I knew I'd found my Forever Home." He wagged his tail. "Reckon it might take a bit longer, but you'll get adopted, I'm sure."

The black puppy perked up and wagged his tail too. "Really? Do you think so?"

"Sure I do," said Ruffster.

"So this scary dog," said Suka impatiently, "what did he look like?"

The black puppy looked at them blankly. "He was scary."

"What colour was he?"

"Black."

"And...?"

The black puppy looked confused. "He was scary."

"But scary like what?" demanded Suka.

The black puppy shrank away. "I... I don't know." He stared at her, his muzzle trembling, and wailed, "*You're* scary!"

"Oh, for kibble's sake!" Suka growled.

"Yer scaring the pup," growled Tyson. "Leave him alone."

"How about the other animals? Maybe they saw something that night?" Biscuit spoke up. He was sitting next to a bin full of pig ears and from the soggy stumps around him had obviously been helping himself. His belly looked bigger than ever. But now he was looking across at the hutches. A little face peered back at them through the mesh, its beady black eyes nearly covered by the huge Mohawk of spiky orange hair on its head.

Ruffster followed his gaze and laughed. "A guinea pig? You serious, mate? You're goin' to try talkin' to a guinea pig?"

Biscuit shrugged a bit sheepishly, but Honey walked across to the hutches.

"Aw, c'mon!" Ruffster followed her over and looked at the guinea pig too. "Honey, you've got to be jokin'. I mean, they probably don't even speak Dog!"

"Maybe we could try speaking their way—" Honey ventured.

"What?" barked Ruffster.

"Yeah, you know humans learn to speak in different ways," said Biscuit. "Frisky the Poodle told me she used to live in a faraway place called Japan and the humans bark totally different there, so her people learnt to bark that way too."

"Yes," said Honey. "Just because other animals speak Dog to us doesn't mean... Well, don't you ever wonder sometimes how to speak like them?"

"No!" laughed Ruffster. "'Course not! Everybody speaks Dog—it's the only way to talk! We're Man's Best Friend and Dog is the Universal Domestic Tongue, so why do we have to worry about speakin' like the other animals?"

"Well, it's nice to learn a bit sometimes." Honey looked down at her paws.

"Aw, for barkin' out loud!" Ruffster rolled his eyes. "Next you'll be tellin' me we should learn to speak Cat!"

"I speak a bit of Cat," growled Tyson. "Want to know what those sly moggers are saying behind my back. Especially the one I live with."

Ruffster shook his head in disbelief and disgust.

"Well, does anybody know how to speak Guinea Pig?" asked Suka with an impatient flick of her tail. "Otherwise, we're just wasting—"

"QUAAAAWWK!"

The dogs all jumped and whirled around. There was a rustling behind them, then a shrill voice came out of the darkness:

"Who dares enter and deviously creep,
Impudent chatter, disturbing my sleep?"

CHAPTER 14

Honey felt all the hackles rise on her back. She sniffed the air, straining her eyes to see. Something tall loomed in the darkness behind them. The rustling again, then the strong *flap-flap-flap* of wings and a gust of air blew in Honey's face, bringing with it the whiff of musty feathers and sunflower seeds.

Her eyes slowly made sense of the darkness and she realised that it was a big parrot perched on a tall stand, watching them. It had a wickedly sharp, hooked black beak, bare white patches around each eye, speckled grey feathers covering its body, and a short tail of fiery crimson. It arched its neck and gave a loud squawk again, causing all the dogs to take a step backwards.

"It's just some stupid bird," said Ruffster, recovering.

"Stupid!" said the parrot in Ruffster's voice.

"Hey!" Ruffster growled, turning towards the parrot.

"Oh, be careful," cried the black puppy

from the pen. "Don't get too close—she's got a nasty bite!"

Ruffster paused, then stuck his head out and sniffed cautiously. The grey parrot leaned down from her perch and tilted her head to one side, looking Ruffster in the eye. Then she whistled suddenly and said in a deep voice, "*Here, boy!*" It sounded so realistic that Ruffster jumped and looked around wildly for his Guy. The grey parrot bobbed up and down on her perch, hooting with laughter.

"Ha! Ha! Ha! Ha! Ha! Ha!"

"You... you toothless turkey! I'll turn you into pillow stuffin'!" Ruffster snarled. He lunged, snapping at empty air as the parrot rose off her perch, flapping her wings and screeching loudly. All the other cages in the shop began to shake and rattle as the mice squeaked, the rabbits thumped, the guinea pigs scratched on the mesh, and the other birds chirped and flapped in alarm.

"Ruffster, stop! STOP!" Honey begged. "You're making too much noise!"

The grey parrot landed back on the perch and smoothed her wings down, then fished a sprig of millet out of her bowl with one foot and began nibbling it.

Ruffster gave her a disgusted look and turned away. "Ah, forget it... Just a waste o' time anyway—"

"You seek answers, good hounds."

All the dogs froze, then looked at the parrot.

"Did the parrot speak to us?" whispered

Suka.

"Parrots don't really talk," scoffed Ruffster. "They just copy sounds, that's all."

"You do me grievous wrong, young mutt. Many tongues I know, including your own," said the parrot in fluent Dog.

Ruffster gaped at the bird.

"Can you help us?" Honey approached the parrot eagerly. "Were you here the night those puppies got taken? Did you see what happened?"

The big grey parrot tilted her head. *"What is not the question."*

"Huh?" said Ruffster. "What is *what*?"

"That makes no sense," said Suka.

"What did ya expect?" growled Tyson. "There's a reason they call them birdbrains."

Honey furrowed her brow, her mind whirling. She stared at the parrot. *What is not the question... What is not the question...* Yes, of course! The question!

"It's the wrong question, isn't it?" she said to the parrot. "We shouldn't be asking 'what', we should be asking something else, like... like 'why'! *Why* were the puppies taken?"

The big grey bird flapped her wings. *"Well done, great hound. Every mystery can be unlocked with a key."*

"So why?" demanded Ruffster. "Why were they taken?"

"It's for dogfighting, isn't it?" asked Suka. "And Max the Pit Bull and his Old Man— they're in on it, aren't they?"

The big grey parrot cocked her head at them. *"To another you must speak, to find the answers you seek."*

"Who?" asked Honey. "Who do we need to speak to? Can you tell us?"

"Perhaps." She sounded amused. She regarded Honey silently for a moment, then extended a foot. *"Sphinx be my name, riddles are my game."*

"Riddles? What's that?" asked Ruffster.

"They're like puzzles," said Suka. "My Boy likes them. He's got a big book full of riddles."

Sphinx the Parrot ruffled her feathers and fixed them all with her beady eye. *"Those deemed worthy of my advice must pass the test and pay the price. Before Knowledge can quench your thirst, my riddle you must answer first."*

"Oh my Dog, this is just like this movie I was watching with my Boy the other day!" gushed Suka. "We have to guess the answer to a riddle and if we get it right, then the parrot will help us!"

Tyson grunted. "Better hurry, though. Ya looked out the window? It's light outside."

The others followed his gaze to the windows at the front of the pet store where the sky was showing pale blue now, streaked with bands of yellow and orange. Dawn was quickly dissolving into a bright morning. Honey didn't know when the humans would come to open up the pet shop, but she guessed that it would be early. They didn't have much time.

"OK," she said, turning back to Sphinx. "What's the riddle?"

The parrot blinked at them, then recited:

"Venture too close and you'll disappear,
Though rats and rabbits have nothing to fear,
The light of day I'll never know,
The more you take, the bigger I grow.
What am I?"

The dogs stared at each other, dumbfounded. Suka repeated the riddle softly to herself, her blue eyes thoughtful. Biscuit stopped chewing and sniffed the air as if hoping to find the answer there.

"That's a riddle?" said Ruffster. "But... that's just a bunch o' gibberish!"

"It's a puzzle. You're supposed to guess the answer. The words are clues and you have to work it out," explained Suka. "That second line, for example—*rats and rabbits have nothing to fear*... So the answer is something that rats and rabbits aren't afraid of."

"They aren't afraid of a lot of things," pointed out Biscuit. "How do we know which one?"

"It's also something that makes you disappear," said Honey, thinking of the first line.

"Foxes?" suggested Biscuit.

"Foxes don't make you disappear," scoffed Ruffster.

"They can if they eat you," said Biscuit. "Foxes eat rabbits."

Ruffster rolled his eyes. "Why does everythin' end up bein' about the stomach with you? Besides, the riddle says rats and rabbits *have nothing to fear,* so it's somethin' they're *not* scared of. Rabbits are scared of foxes, so that can't be the answer. "

"What about the last line?" Tyson growled. "About growing bigger?"

"The more you take, the bigger I grow," mused Suka. "But things usually get *smaller* when you take more away!"

"OK, what about the part about never seein' the *light o' day?*" said Ruffster. "Reckon it's an animal that only comes out at night?"

"Owl?" suggested Tyson. "Bats? Fireflies?"

"But they don't grow bigger when you take more away," said Suka, frowning.

"I know, I know!" said Biscuit excitedly. "Maybe never knowing the light of day means something underground! Like... like a carrot! Rabbits love carrots, so they wouldn't be scared of that."

"Carrots don't make ya disappear," growled Tyson.

Biscuit sat back, crestfallen.

Honey gave his ear a lick. "The underground idea was a good one, Biscuit." She shifted her weight, aware of the throbbing in her front paw again. The numbness had spread higher, all the way up to her elbow now. She didn't want to look to see where the lump was. She could feel it moving—tugging, squirming, wriggling—under her skin.

Hurriedly, she turned her attention back to the riddle, the words circling in her head. There was something about that last line, she thought: *The more you take, the bigger I grow.*

But Suka was right, how could anything grow bigger when you took more away? And yet... something nagged at the edge of her mind.

"I got it!" Ruffster bounced like a puppy. "It's those tall black hats humans wear!"

Suka looked at him blankly. "Black hats?"

"Yeah, yeah," said Ruffster, pacing with excitement. "I saw them on the TV box with my Guy. There was this man and he pulled a rabbit out from inside one o' those hats. And then he put a white bird inside and made it disappear! See? Just like in the riddle." He paused and added. "And the hat's black— which is the opposite of light, right? That fits in with not knowin' the *light o' day*."

"But what about the growing bigger bit?" asked Biscuit.

"Oh, who cares? The rest o' it fits," said Ruffster, turning to the parrot. "C'mon, Sphinx—am I right? Is that the answer?"

The big grey parrot chuckled, swaying from side to side on her perch. *"Guess on, young mutt, for your answer is wrong. But hurry you must, for you haven't got long."*

The dogs all jumped as an engine rumbled to life in the square outside. Honey glanced towards the front of the store. Rays of sunshine were filtering in the front windows and she could make out movement through the glass and hear voices outside. The square was coming to life.

"We're going to get caught if we don't leave soon," said Suka.

Honey looked pleadingly at the parrot. "Can't you just tell us the answer?"

Sphinx paused in preening her feathers and raised her head. *"Rules are rules, no exceptions are made. Answer my riddle or forfeit my trade."*

"Aw, c'mon, you feather windbag!" Ruffster growled. "Look, mate, we've tried real hard to guess, all right? But we just can't think o' the answer and we haven't got the time to keep standin' around here guessin'!"

A thump came from outside the front door of the pet shop. Footsteps. Then the dogs heard talking and laughter.

"Howling hyenas, it's the shop people!" said Suka.

"C'mon, c'mon... we've got to go!" Ruffster nudged Honey's shoulder with his nose. "They'll be in here any minute!"

"But..." Honey hesitated. "But we can't! We haven't—"

"There's no time!"

Tyson picked up the dead scarab in his mouth and started towards the back room. Biscuit gave the treat bin a wistful look, then turned to follow him. Suka hovered, undecided, her eyes flicking to the front door and back. Ruffster nudged Honey again but she ignored him. She couldn't just give up and leave—she couldn't! She shut her eyes and tried desperately to think.

Ruffster growled in frustration and turned on Suka, hustling the Husky towards the back room, snapping at her heels like his Corgi grandfather when she tried to protest.

"No, wait!" Honey gave her booming Great Dane bark. The deep sound halted everybody

in their tracks. They all stared at her.
    "I know the answer to the riddle!"

CHAPTER 15

Honey turned quickly to the grey parrot and took a deep breath. "The answer is 'hole', isn't it? If you get too close to a hole, you could fall in and disappear... but rabbits and rats live in them, so they have nothing to fear. It's dark in there, so there's no 'light of day'... and most of all... When you're digging a hole, the more soil you take away, the bigger it grows!"

Sphinx gave a screech of excitement and arched her neck, raising the feathers in a ruff and bobbing her head up and down. "*Well played, great hound, now listen well—*"

The jingle of keys from outside made them all jerk their gazes to the front door. They heard an angry mutter as the human fumbled for the right key.

Honey turned back to Sphinx. "Quick! Tell us!"

The grey parrot spread her wings and croaked loudly:

"To old sworn enemies, now you must turn,

*From their ancient knowledge, soon you
must learn,*
  So seek those who prowl with velvet paws,
  And worship a king with deadly claws.

"Chokin' chicken bones!" groaned Ruffster.
"Not another stupid riddle!"

At that moment, they heard the key turn
in the lock and the creak of the front door
hinges.

"Get out! Get out! Now!" Ruffster yelled,
bolting towards the back room. Suka sprang
after him and Honey followed, trying to run
but finding that her whole front leg was
numb. She stumbled, groping for the ground
with a front paw she could no longer feel.

"Honey! Are you OK?" Suka looked back at
her.

"Yes," gulped Honey. "Go! I'm coming!"

The front door swung open and light
flooded the pet shop. Honey heard a cry of
surprise but she didn't look back. She hobbled
towards the back room and stumbled through
the doorway just in time to see Suka's fluffy
tail disappear through the gap under the
roller door. She threw herself across the room
and wriggled into the opening.

"Hurry, Honey!" Ruffster urged from the
other side.

Honey shoved with her back legs and felt
the roller door scrape painfully along her
back, then with a creak and rattle that shook
the whole metal frame, she was through. She
stood up shakily.

"Come on!" Suka called from further down

the alleyway. "This side leads out onto another street, away from the square!"

The dogs all bolted after her with Honey hobbling at the rear. Behind them, they heard muffled shouts from the pet shop, but when Honey glanced over her shoulder, she saw nobody chasing them. It looked like they were safe. Still, they didn't stop until they were several blocks away and then finally paused, gasping and panting, in the shade of a large tree.

"Did you hear it? Did you all hear the second riddle?" asked Honey, panting.

Suka nodded. "I've been repeating it to myself while I was running so I wouldn't forget."

"What do you think it m—"

"Hey," Ruffster interrupted Honey. "You're not going to start guessin' that stupid riddle now? Here?"

"Yeah, we should really find somewhere to hide and rest first," agreed Suka, licking her sore paw pads and looking around at the others. Tyson sat panting, the dead scarab he had been carrying by his feet, and Biscuit was sprawled next to him, looking exhausted.

"But where? A group o' dogs like us—ain't no way people won't notice us. And I don't know about you, but I reckon my Guy's reported my escape by now and called the Dog Catcher," said Ruffster.

Biscuit roused himself. "We're near the school," he said, sniffing the air.

Suka perked up, looking around. "Yes, we're near my Boy's school! I know somewhere we can hide! There's an old shed at the back of his school playground. Nobody ever goes there. We'll be safe there for a while."

"Lead the way!" said Ruffster, his tail wagging.

The sun was seeping through the dirty windows and throwing long shadows across the floor when Honey opened her eyes. For a moment, she wondered where she was. The old burlap sack she was lying on felt scratchy under her body. Above her head, a low ceiling broke the dusty darkness, its wooden beams festooned with old cobwebs. There were several wooden poles propped on the wall beside her. Human tools, she realised. Olivia had some of those for digging up soil and pushing dead leaves around. Then she remembered. They were in the old garden shed at the school.

Honey stretched gingerly, careful not to disturb the other dogs who were all still sleeping. She glanced down at her right front leg, extended at an awkward angle in front of her.

"Honey... what's wrong with your leg?"

Honey turned to see Suka sitting up, looking at her worriedly. The others were stirring too. Ruffster yawned and scratched his upright ear while Tyson stood up, stretching. Biscuit groaned and rolled over, and a tinkle of music drifted from his stomach.

"I don't know," Honey said. "I...I think I got bitten by one of the scarabs."

"You what?" Ruffster paused mid-scratch. The others were all wide awake now, staring at her. "Why didn't you tell us, mate?"

"I was scared," said Honey in a small voice. "I thought... maybe I was just imagining things or... or it would go away."

Biscuit crept forwards to sniff her leg. His nose twitched as he came near the lump, which was now jutting out from under Honey's elbow. He jerked back as if he had been burnt. "There's... there's something *alive* in there."

"Howling hyenas...," said Suka. "Honey! Remember the curse? What it said about the *black hunger... consume from within...*" She stared in horror at the lump as it squirmed suddenly under Honey's skin. "That's... that's probably a scarab inside you, eating you alive!"

"No!" Honey tucked her tail between her legs. "I don't even feel any pain anymore. It hurt a lot more in the beginning, but now it's just sort of numb."

Suka's blue eyes opened even wider. "That's *exactly* what some bugs do to you! I read about it in one of my Boy's science books! There's a kind of wasp that makes its babies grow inside other bugs, and they use this creepy insect drool to paralyse their victims so they don't feel anything while the baby wasps are eating them up from the inside."

Honey shivered, wishing Suka would stop

talking. Ruffster stared at the lump under Honey's skin, then at the dead scarab on the ground next to him. It was the beetle the puppy had shown them in the pet shop. They had been taking it in turns to carry it with them.

Ruffster shifted uneasily. "Maybe you should go home, mate, and get the Pet Sitter to take you to the vet—"

"No," said Honey.

"But—"

"I'm not going home." Honey took a deep breath. "Vets won't know how to deal with this. It isn't like some tick bite. Those scarabs... this curse... it's all linked to the mystery of the missing puppies, so the best thing for me is to find the puppies."

"You could show them the dead one we have here and—"

Honey growled. "No! Let's just try to solve the second riddle, OK?"

The others nodded, surprised by her uncharacteristic forcefulness. Honey turned to Suka and asked the Husky to recite the riddle.

"To old sworn enemies, now you must turn," quoted Suka softly. *"From their ancient knowledge, soon you must learn."*

"But we don't have any enemies," said Biscuit in a puzzled voice. "I mean, I don't like some of the dogs down at the park, but I wouldn't call any of them enemies..."

"Maybe it's talkin' about the enemies o' all dogs," suggested Ruffster. "Like, what are the worst things for dogs?"

"Baths," said Honey with a shudder.

"Nail clippers!" growled Tyson.

"Diets," muttered Biscuit.

"Stupid recalls," said Suka.

"Cats!" said Ruffster. "No bigger enemy than that bunch o' sneaky, sardine-breathed sand poopers."

Suka sighed. "Now, Ruffster, just because you've got an issue with cats—"

"No, wait... I think he's right," said Honey. "My human, Olivia, says dogs and cats are so famous as enemies that humans even have a special saying about them: 'fighting like cats and dogs'. And cats might have some ancient knowledge that could help us."

"Ancient knowledge? My paw!" sneered Ruffster.

"Yeah." Tyson looked doubtful. "I live with a cat and the only ancient knowledge she's got is where she buried her poo in the litter tray yesterday."

"OK, what about the second part of the riddle?" said Suka. "The bit about *seek those who prowl with velvet paws.*"

"*And worship a king with deadly claws.*" Honey finished it for her.

"Well, I reckon prowlin' with velvet paws would still point to cats," said Ruffster.

"And the *king with deadly claws?*"

Tyson gave a bark of laughter. "Deadly claws? More like a deadly bum! Always shoving it in yer face—"

"Yeah, mate," said Ruffster. "The only deadly thin' about any cat I've met is its Kitty Stink!"

"What about that black one we met behind Max's house?" Biscuit spoke up. "She was pretty deadly. She nearly took my head off!"

"That's because she was a feral," protested Ruffster.

"Wait," said Suka. "That's it! That's the answer to the riddle! We've got to go to the feral cat colony. They're the only ones who would have *ancient knowledge*—they still know all the old stories the pet kitties have forgotten."

"Feral cat colony?" said Honey uneasily.

Suka nodded excitedly. "I've heard about it but I thought it was just a story—you know, like the giant peanut-butter bone at the end of the rainbow or the moon being made of liver... but no, this must be true. They say there's a great feral cat colony on the other side of the cemetery. It's been there, like, long before any of us was born." Suka dropped her voice. "And they have this leader—a huge cat with deadly claws who can kill in a single swipe. They call him Jack the Ripper. They say no dog who has gone there has ever come back."

CHAPTER 16

They set off just after sundown, slipping out of the shed and making their way cautiously through the school playgrounds. Biscuit ran in loops around the other dogs, his nose to the ground, searching for scraps of food dropped by the children. Honey's stomach rumbled as she listened to Biscuit describe a piece of cream cake smeared on a bench. None of them had eaten breakfast that morning and after a whole day without food, listening to Biscuit talk about sausage rolls and jam doughnuts wasn't helping their mood any.

"Will ya shut up?" growled Tyson. "If you say one more thing about leftover sandwiches, I'll eat ya myself!"

"This way," called Suka, already by the school gates. "There's a shortcut to the cemetery down those streets."

"The cemetery?" Biscuit stopped in mid-sniff.

Ruffster shifted his mouth around the dead scarab he was carrying. "I'm not goin' back in there," he declared. "Not for all the bones in Mexico!"

"The feral cat colony is on the other side," said Suka. "If we don't go through the cemetery, then we'll have to go around it."

"Let's do that," said Biscuit quickly and Tyson nodded agreement.

Honey said nothing, focusing all her energy on keeping up with the others. She was limping noticeably now and her right front leg dragged uselessly along as she used her three good legs to hobble forwards. She trailed behind the other dogs as they crossed several streets, making their way to the cemetery. Twice Biscuit scented the Dog Catcher and once Ruffster saw his black jeep, fitted with the rattling cages at the back, parked around a street corner, but they managed to avoid being seen.

Finally they were back in the alley behind Max's house. Honey glanced at the bins further up the alley, but there was no feline shape in the shadows today. They could easily see where the feral cat might have gone, though: the alley ended at the cemetery wall and beyond it, as the cemetery wall veered away, they could see dense woodland. The only way to get to the other side of the cemetery was to go through those woods and follow the curve of the cemetery wall until they circled around to the other side.

"Er... reckon this is a good idea?" asked Ruffster, scratching his ear nervously.

The entrance into the woods was screened by thick bushes, and flickering shadows moved through the trees beyond. The air smelled damp and alive with things that crawled and rustled. Biscuit went forwards and sniffed around the bushes, then suddenly disappeared into them.

"Biscuit?" Ruffster hovered after him.

"In here!"

They crowded closer. Now they could see the grass between the bushes had been trampled down by feet and paws and that a trail led into the undergrowth beyond.

Biscuit was already further along the trail, nosing something on the ground. "Look what I found!" There was a rustle of plastic and the sounds of munching. "Come on! There's enough here for everybody!"

One by one, the other dogs slipped through the gap in the bushes to join Biscuit. Honey was the last and as she started to push her way into the bushes, she paused. Something stirred behind her and she felt her hackles rise. She whirled around... but there was nothing there. She looked down the alley, puzzled, lifting her nose to scent the air. There had definitely been something there.

Something... someone... watching her...

She peered into the gathering dark but the alley was still and silent.

"Honey! What are you doin'?"

"Come on! Hurry up!"

Honey threw one more glance around her, then turned and pushed her way into the bushes to join the others. They were gathered around Biscuit and his find—a big plastic bag filled with half-eaten sandwiches. Honey lowered her head and scooped up a sandwich, sinking her teeth into the soft bread. *Mmm*. It was peanut butter and jelly. The sweet, nutty flavours oozed in her mouth and drool dribbled down her chin.

"Honey!" Tyson growled, edging away from her. "Keep yer slobber to yerself!"

"Sorry!" Honey swallowed and licked her jowls.

"What's all this food doing here?" asked Suka, licking peanut butter off her nose.

Biscuit swallowed. "Humans always throw rubbish wherever they go. You won't believe the perfectly good stuff they throw away. That's what the Beagle Brigade specialises in. We're not just any scavengers, you know. We perform an important social service by helping to find and clean up human waste."

Suka rolled her eyes. The plastic bag was almost empty now. Honey licked up the last of the bread crumbs and turned to follow the others as they continued on the trail. She felt better now with some food in her stomach, and she tried to hobble faster. Still, it was hard to keep up on three legs. Besides... she let the others go ahead as she paused again and looked over her shoulder. There it was, that feeling again. Like somebody watching her. She scented the air and scanned the trail behind her but saw nothing, smelled nothing. She shook her head. *This is stupid.*

Honey was just about to turn and hurry after the others when a shape detached itself from the deeper shadows of the bushes behind her. Moonlight fell onto a scarred, grizzled muzzle. She inhaled sharply as she realised who it was. Max the Pit Bull.

"You're following me!" she said.

Max stepped closer. "I caught your scent as you were all passing my house." He cocked his head. "Where are you going?"

Honey felt a flash of anger as she remembered his response when she had asked him about the bundle yesterday. "It's none of your business," she said nastily. Then, before she could stop herself, she blurted, "Was it you? In the cemetery?"

"Cemetery?" Max looked wary.

"Yes, I saw your paw prints," Honey said in a rush, suddenly glad to have it all out in the open. "With the puppy ones."

"I was never in the cemetery," said Max.

"But I saw them! The paw prints with three toes—that must have been you!" Honey glanced down at his front paws.

Max followed her gaze. In the light of the full moon filtering down through the trees around them, they could see his left paw clearly. There were only three toes. Where the fourth toe should have been was only a scarred stump.

CHAPTER 17

"Yes, I lost that toe... a long time ago," said Max slowly. "But I wasn't in the cemetery with the puppies. That paw print wasn't from me."

"But—" Honey broke off as she heard Ruffster's voice coming from the trail ahead of them.

"Hey, Honey, you all right? If you're havin' trouble keepin' up, you should've tol—" Ruffster emerged, carrying the scarab in his mouth. He saw Max and his voice turned cold. He dropped the scarab on the ground. "Oh. It's you."

The others followed, coming back to see what the delay was. Tyson's hackles began bristling as soon as he saw Max.

"What are ya doing here?" he snarled, baring his teeth.

Max stiffened and the muscles in his shoulders rippled. Honey saw Suka's eyes widen with anticipation and she realised that any minute there would be a dogfight. A nasty, vicious, bloody dogfight.

"Come on, we have to go," she said gently, moving to stand between Max and Tyson. "We haven't got much time."

Tyson gave a growl but he grudgingly took a step back. Max didn't move but the hard look faded from his eyes and his tail relaxed. For a moment, Tyson looked like he was going to say something else, then he turned with a grunt and trotted away down the trail, his hackles still up in a stiff ridge along his back.

"Where are you going?" Max asked again.

"What's it to you?" snapped Ruffster.

"I know you're looking for the missing puppies—" Max began.

"So?" Ruffster interrupted. "Why should we tell you anythin'?

"I might be able to help."

Suka thrust her nose into Max's face. "We don't need help from Pit Bulls." She turned, flicking her tail across his face, and walked off down the trail. Biscuit gave a contemptuous snort in Max's direction and followed.

"C'mon, Honey," said Ruffster, giving Max a dirty look and turning away. He picked up the dead scarab again and trotted down the trail.

Honey started to follow them, but her steps faltered. She looked back. Max stood on the trail behind them, watching them go. Moonlight slid over the muscles of his body, outlining him in silver. It was as if Honey was seeing him for the first time, and what she saw was not a vicious monster, a savage killer... instead, she saw a dog that stood alone. Always alone. Ostracised. Outcast. Feared and hated. Bearing always the spite and blame of others.

Suddenly she didn't want to be part of that anymore.

She took a few steps back towards Max and said, "We're going to the feral cat colony. They might know something that can help us find the puppies."

There were angry gasps from further down the trail when the other dogs heard her, but Honey ignored them. Surprise and some other emotion she couldn't name flickered in Max's dark eyes. Without waiting to see what he might do, Honey turned and hobbled to join the others.

"Festering fleas, Honey, are ya crazy?" Tyson demanded as soon as she had caught up with them.

"Yeah, Honey, he might be involved, you know. Maybe he's tryin' to stop us findin' the pups," Ruffster said, falling into step beside her.

"He's not," said Honey. "I...I can't explain it but I know he's *good.*"

"Good? A Pit Bull?" said Suka with a laugh. "OK, Honey, I know you Danes are all great big softies but seriously, even you can't be that naïve. He could be—"

"Shh!" said Biscuit suddenly, up ahead. He was standing with one paw raised, sniffing the air uneasily.

Honey realised they had come much further than they'd thought while they were talking. The cemetery wall was now curving away behind them—they had gone around it and were now on the other side. In front of them, the trees thinned and the woods opened out into a clearing. Moonlight swept over the open space, giving everything an eerie glow.

An old house stood on the far side of the clearing, surrounded by weeds and overgrown bushes. Barbed wire snaked along the ground around it and an old sign hung from a rope across the front door. Its surface was scratched and faded, but Honey could just make out the words: *DANGER! KEEP OUT!*

"It's a human place," said Suka in a hushed voice. "Though it looks like nobody's been here for a long time."

Honey followed her gaze up to the darkened windows, many smashed and gaping open, the glass shards forming jagged rows along the window frames. It gave the disturbing illusion of many mouths with rows of teeth, all open towards them. Honey shivered.

They went forwards slowly across the clearing, their paws sinking in the damp grass. Despite the brightness of the moon above, the night seemed to close around them like a thick glove. Honey felt the hairs along her back stand up, and she could see both Tyson's and Ruffster's hackles bristling too.

They paused just outside the front door and pricked their ears, listening. There was nothing except the faint chirp of crickets in the woods behind them and somewhere closer, the *tup-tup-tup* of water dripping.

"I don't like this place." Biscuit shivered.

"It's just a stupid old house," said Ruffster. He dropped the scarab he had been carrying and raised his nose to sniff the air. "Don't smell anythin'."

"The wind's in the wrong direction," said Biscuit, looking around uneasily. "It's blowing our scent towards the house but we can't smell anything from inside."

Ruffster gave an impatient growl. "Well, I'm not scared o' a bunch o' cats." He approached the front windows. Tyson picked up the dropped scarab and they reluctantly followed him. They watched as Ruffster hitched his paws up against the wall and stood up on his hind legs to look into one of the broken windows.

He dropped back to the ground, disappointed. "Nothin'." He looked up at the house again, then let out a couple of loud barks.

"Ruffster!" hissed Suka. "What are you doing?"

He turned to Suka in disgust. "There's no one here," he said. "Reckon it's just some dumb story after all. There's this old house sittin' here, so they start makin' up stuff about a feral cat colony."

"No," said Suka, looking around nervously. "It's not just a made-up story."

"Well, where are all the cats, then?" said Ruffster. "There's not so much as a sniff o' a hairball. I can't believe we're standin' here scared—for kibble's sake, we're dogs, remember? Cats run from us!"

Biscuit made a funny sound, his nose quivering, and looked up. The others all raised their heads as well. On the roof above them, several dark shapes appeared. They stood like statues, silhouetted against the night sky, long tails flicking. Then, one by one, they dropped like plummeting shadows to the ground and encircled the dogs, their eyes glittering.

CHAPTER 18

Ten dark wraiths surrounded them, silent, waiting. The moonlight gleamed on their pelts, showing them not to be solid black, but thickly striped and marbled. *They're all tabbies*, Honey thought, her mind scrabbling like a wild animal and clutching on to that irrelevant fact. Then she saw something else that made her breath catch in her throat. Their claws. Each cat unsheathed a set of claws that curved like wicked talons.

"Oh my Dog," squeaked Biscuit, staring at the claws. "There's blood on them!"

Honey followed his gaze and saw the dark red tips of some of the claws. Her stomach clenched. She felt the others stiffen beside her. The dogs edged closer together, rumps touching, facing out towards the ring of cats.

"Tyson, you speak Cat," whispered Suka. "Ask them what they want."

Tyson dropped the scarab beetle he had been carrying and eyed the claws. "Ya don't need to know Cat to know what they're thinking," he muttered.

"P...please," Honey said, her voice quavering. "We're not here to make trouble. We need your help."

The cats said nothing. They sat, staring, extending and retracting those terrible claws, their tails flicking occasionally. It was unnerving.

"This is stupid," growled Ruffster. "Told you—there's only one way to deal with these fleabags!" And he rushed at one of the cats, barking loudly in its face.

The big grey tabby didn't even flinch. Ruffster faltered, suddenly unsure. He'd met cats who ran and he'd met cats who hissed and spat in his face, but he'd never before met a cat who did nothing but stare. His tail dropped between his legs and he scrambled to retreat, whining in confusion. As he pushed his way back into the huddle of dogs, one paw knocked against the dead scarab, kicking it outwards. The beetle skidded out into the open space and moonlight fell on the shiny black shell, picking out tones of purple and blue and making the scarab look for a moment more like a sinister jewel than a dead beetle.

The effect on the cats was electrifying. They sprang up, their eyes on the scarab, their ears flattened and whiskers quivering. Their smooth tabby coats were now spiked and bristling.

"Where did you get that?" The grey tabby hissed.

He reached forwards but Honey was quicker. Before anyone realised what she was doing, she had lunged forwards to stand over the scarab. The iridescent sheen of the black shell disappeared under her huge Great Dane paw. She looked up, straight into the green eyes of the grey tabby.

"Release it, dog."

Honey blanched. She was close enough to count his whiskers, feel his musky odour invading her nostrils. Drool flooded her mouth in a panicked gush. All she wanted to do was turn tail and run. But she stood her ground.

"N...no." Honey gulped. "We... we need to see your king... um... leader, I mean. I will only give it to him."

The grey tabby slowly unsheathed his claws. Honey stared at their crimson tips. She felt her muscles tense, and she wondered wildly if there was any way she could move fast enough to avoid those slashing talons.

Then the claws disappeared into grey fur. "Come." The big grey tabby turned with a flick of his tail and padded away.

Honey stood frozen for a moment, her heart still pounding, the drool dangling from her jowls—then she shook herself, causing the cats nearby to jump back from the shower of slobber. She picked up the scarab and started after the grey tabby. Behind her, she heard the other dogs scrabbling to accompany her. She followed the grey tabby around the side of the house to the back. There had once been a vegetable garden here, it seemed, but it had since grown wild and any vegetables were lost now in the tangle of weeds and grasses.

The grey tabby disappeared into a towering bush, which seemed to have grown straight into the back wall of the house. Looking closer, Honey realised that it in fact concealed a huge gap where the crumbling wall had fallen away. She hesitated for a moment, then plunged through, dragging her numb front leg beside her. A thorn stabbed into her side and she flinched, feeling several more pierce her fur before she managed to wriggle through. Behind her, she heard the yelps and grunts of the other dogs as they followed her.

Finally, they were all through. They stood, panting, looking around what used to be a huge old kitchen. A gnarled wooden table still stood in the corner, and next to it, a chair lay overturned on the floor, one wooden leg missing. On the far wall, the sooty mouth of an empty fireplace yawned and beside it a long counter, its tiled surface cracked and chipped, ran the length of the room, ending in a big metal sink.

And there were cats—cats of every size, shape and colour; cats everywhere: on the table and underneath, surrounding the fireplace, huddled on the counter, peering over the edge of the sink, scooting along the walls, peeking from behind the ripped chair seat, watching from the cobwebbed shelves that lined the walls. It felt like a hundred yellow and green eyes were watching them, and the pungent smell of Kitty Odour was overwhelming.

Honey swallowed down a wave of nausea, feeling her old cat phobia rise in her throat. Outside, things had happened too fast for her to think much about it, but now she was horribly aware of how many cats were around her, how close they all were. She had to fight the urge to dive back through that gap and run back into the woods. It almost made her laugh at her fear over that one little kitten in the tree.

As if following her thoughts, a trio of kittens tumbled out suddenly in front of her. They froze and stared up at her, eyes wide, little tails straight out like stiff brushes. The fear in their eyes made Honey forget her own, and she lowered her head towards them, reaching out tentatively with her nose.

A sudden yowl made her spring back. A ginger-and-white cat shot out of nowhere and stood over the kittens, her lips curling back to show her fangs. She narrowed her eyes into slits. "Stay away from my kittens, *ya kaalb*."

Honey dipped her head and averted her eyes, edging away. She glanced back at Ruffster, half expecting him to charge forwards with his usual kitty-hating enthusiasm, but the mongrel mutt had his ears and tail down, his eyes subdued. She wondered if the encounter with the grey tabby outside had scared him more than he wanted to admit.

Thoughts of the grey tabby reminded Honey of why they were in here. She looked around and saw the big grey cat heading towards the fireplace. He threw a look back, obviously expecting them to follow, and she limped after him. She saw as she neared the fireplace that it was being used as a sort of den. A pair of eyes watched, unblinking, from the shadowed recesses as she approached. Honey tried not to stare but she had never seen eyes like that before. One was a brilliant green and the other was a deep amber.

The shadows moved and a cat stepped out. A tom with a massive head that echoed the majesty of a lion stood looking at them silently. His brown tabby coat was punctured with scars and one of his ears was nothing more than ragged shreds of skin, but there was no doubting the power in that thick, muscular body. He flexed his front paws, and suddenly, Honey could see nothing else except his claws. Huge, black talons that curved into lethal points, they made the ones on the grey tabby look like kitten's nails. No normal cat claws looked like that. These claws were made to maim and kill.

She heard Suka breathe beside her: "So it's true..." and the other dogs crowded closer together. Honey fought down another wave of nausea and took a trembling step forwards.

CHAPTER 19

"Are... are you the one they call J...Jack the Ripper?"

The great brown tabby fixed those startling, mismatched eyes on her. Honey forced herself to meet them.

"I am he." He inclined his head. Like the other cats, he spoke Dog fluently but with a strange, guttural accent. "Jack is my name when I walk the streets of Man. Here, I am known by my feline name... Jahi." He sat and wrapped his tail around his front paws, covering those terrible claws. He looked over at the grey tabby, then back at them, narrowing his eyes. "Tor tells me that you seek our help."

Taking a deep breath, Honey explained about the missing puppies and the words of Sphinx the Parrot. "She told us to come to you. She said you had 'ancient wisdom' which could help us."

"Our 'ancient wisdom', as you call it, is ours to keep. It is not something to be shared with others—especially not with *kaalb*."

"But—"

"However," he continued, "we always honour a debt of gratitude. You rescued a kitten and brought it to its mother, one of our queens. Nathifa speaks highly of you." He looked across the room.

Honey followed his gaze across to one of the shelves on the wall where a slim tortoiseshell cat sat watching them. A little bundle of black fur was curled up against her side. She blinked at Honey in affection and recognition. Honey wagged her tail in return.

She turned hopefully back to the great brown tabby. "So you'll help us?"

Jack raised one paw and washed it slowly, unsheathing those deadly claws and flexing each one. The dogs watched with bated breath. Finally he lowered his paw. "You carry with you a beetle of darkness." His eyes went to the scarab on the ground by Honey's paws.

Honey carefully pushed the dead beetle into the space between them. The faint moonlight coming in through the kitchen windows played over the iridescence of the black shell again and traced the lines of the marks etched on its surface. The great brown tabby blinked and the tip of his tail began twitching, but otherwise he made no movement.

"They found one of these left behind whenever a puppy disappeared. What does it mean?" asked Honey. "Outside, Tor and the other cats—they all jumped up when they saw it."

Jack looked down at the scarab shell. "The pictures... they are an ancient language."

"Yes, we know. They're hieroglyphics. They spell *Inpw*," said Honey, catching Suka's eye as she remembered the word the Husky had decoded from the chart in her Boy's book. The same word which had been repeated over and over on that strange memorial stone in the cemetery.

Jack looked up at her, then at the other dogs, and Honey saw surprise and respect in his eyes.

He nodded. "Yes, it spells a name; *Inpw*— or *Anpu* or *Anubis* as he is sometimes known—is their master. The beetles of darkness follow his command—they guard for him, kill for him, and they are always with him; they cling to him and feed from him, like unearthly fleas."

"Like fleas...? You mean *Inpw* is a dog?" Honey thought suddenly of the puppy in the pet shop and his story of a "scary dog".

Jack looked steadily at her. "Yes, he is a *kaalb*—a dog—but not a dog of flesh like you and your friends. He answers not to Man but to another, from ancient times, and the territory he guards is the realms of *Duat*."

"*Duat*?" Honey cocked her head.

"The Underworld of Old Egypt."

"He's a ghost dog?"

Jack shrugged. "Ghost is a human word. It is limited, like the human mind. It is a poor word for something that is both more and less. It is better to say, perhaps, that *Inpw* is a dog of another world. An ancient world from another time."

"So how come we've never heard o' him?" Ruffster spoke up.

The great brown tabby turned his green-amber eyes to the other dogs. "There are not many among you dogs who remember the old stories. In your allegiance to Man, you have abandoned much of the ancient knowledge along with your instincts and your freedom. But we cats are different. We may share Man's home, but we still remember a time when we were free."

Jack narrowed his eyes. "And we know the truth about the old stories—the stories that humans like to change. They are vain, humans—they like to think of all things in their own image. For example, their stories of Old Egypt show *Inpw* as a man with a dog's head—"

"Oh! Yes, I remember that picture in my Boy's book," cried Suka. "A man with the head of a black dog; I thought it was really creepy. He's supposed to lead the dead into the Underworld or something like that." She tilted her head to the side, remembering. "Wasn't there a woman with the head of a cat as well?"

Jack hissed and spat and all the dogs jumped backwards.

"Another lie spread by the vanity of Man!" Jack lashed his tail. "You speak of *Bastet*. She is no woman… she is a cat. However, it was she who first decided to step into the world of Man. It is through her enchantment that cats flourish today—for there is no other animal who lives with Man as cats do. Unlike horses and cows or even you dogs, we need perform no useful function to share his home, to be worshipped and adored."

"Don't look so worshipped and adored livin' here in this dump," muttered Ruffster under his breath.

The great brown tabby looked at him sharply and Ruffster dropped his ears and lowered his head. "Well, I'm just sayin'…"

Jack sat up straighter, a distant look in his eyes. "In the beginning, there was *Sekhmet* the Lioness whose breath created the desert. She was known for her fierceness, her cunning, and her courage in battle. But then she chose the world of Man with its easy food, warm beds, and soft living, and she became *Bastet* the Cat." He turned back to the dogs, one eye brilliant green, the other one glowing amber. "But some of us have the fierceness of *Sekhmet* still in our blood. We choose to live outside Man's shadow—to live harsher lives but to be free."

There was a sudden commotion on the other side of the room. A pale tabby shot in through the gap and rushed up to Jack. Honey watched uneasily as the other cats in the room began to stir restlessly. She saw Nathifa pick up the black kitten by its scruff, hop off the shelf, and disappear into the shadows.

"What's going on?" growled Tyson under his breath.

Jack turned back to them. "There is a man coming through the woods. He holds a light and walks like a hunter searching for prey. We have seen him before. He usually comes in a black machine with cages at the back, and the smell of dog is strong on him."

Suka gasped. "Howling hyenas! The Dog Catcher!"

Jack's eyes glinted in the dark. "He will arrive at the house soon."

CHAPTER 20

"What are we going to do?" asked Biscuit in a scared whisper. "If the Dog Catcher gets us, we'll all end up at the dog pound."

The other dogs shuddered. Tales of the dog pound had scared them since they were puppies suckling at their mothers' sides and the stories of dogs who went there and never came back gave even dogs like Tyson nightmares. Honey eased her weight off her numb front leg. She thought of the Dog Catcher and wondered if she would be able to run fast enough to escape him.

Then she thought of the kittens she had seen earlier. They wouldn't be able to run either. She looked at Jack. "What about the colony?"

The great brown tabby gave his tail a relaxed flick. "It is simple for us to hide; there are many places and we are skilled at evading human hands. But for you," he said, his eyes roving over them, lingering especially on Honey's tall body, "it is not so easy. It would be wise to leave before the man arrives. For you, escape is easier in open spaces."

"But how are we goin' to do that? Our only way back is through the woods," said Ruffster. "We'll be runnin' straight into him."

"There is another way back into town without having to go through the woods. Tor will show you." He nodded at the grey tabby. "It is the longer way to get back to the cemetery, but it would be safer."

"Back to the cemetery?" Honey looked at him in surprise. "But why—"

"It is your only hope of rescuing the puppies," said Jack. "If *Inpw* has taken them, then it is not in this world that you need to seek them."

Suka stared. "Are you saying he's taking the puppies back to the Underworld with him?"

The brown tabby dipped his great head. "Yes. But you may be able to catch up with him before. There are *touch-points* between our world and *Duat*—they are called the *Ka* doors and they are often found in the resting places of the dead. They are guarded by the army of Khepri—the Scarab God."

"Khepri? That was the name on that weird memorial stone! Chokin' chicken bones, when those scarabs attacked us in the cemetery," said Ruffster, "it was 'coz we were gettin' too close to one of these *Ka* doors, weren't we?"

"But what if *Inpw* has taken the puppies into the Underworld already?" Honey said urgently.

Jack blinked. "Then you cannot save them.

The living cannot set foot in the realms of *Duat*. But there is a Place In-Between through which you must travel before you come to the Gates of *Duat*. You may yet have time to save the puppies if you can catch up with them there."

There was still a chance! Honey hardly took in the rest of what he said. All she could think about was that there was still a chance to save Bean and the other puppies. She wagged her tail and turned to Jack eagerly. "So how—"

"Hiyal!"

"Hiyal! Insan!"

A burst of white light sliced in through the kitchen windows. Cats scattered in all directions, eyes wide, fur bristling. The dogs flattened themselves to the floor. The beam roved across the room, casting leering shadows on the kitchen walls. It slid across the counter and over the fireplace, narrowly missing the top of Honey's head before arcing across to the table where it caught several pairs of cat eyes, glittering and opaque. The beam wavered and blinked out.

Honey let out the breath she had been holding and felt the other dogs do the same.

"Can he get in?" she asked Jack who sat placidly beside them, his tail tucked once more around his front paws.

The great brown tabby glanced towards the kitchen windows. "The way through the front of the house is barred. And the only way in here is through that gap in the wall. The thorn bush may deter him—Man has soft skin and gives up easily—but it would not be wise to wait and find out." He stood and stretched, curving his back into a perfect arch, then turned with a flick of his tail. "Come."

He led them across the room to the gap in the wall.

"But…" Honey stopped beside the opening, confused. "You just said this gap is the only way in. Aren't we just heading straight towards him?"

"It is also the only way out," said Jack. "You have no choice."

He looked behind them, his eyes meeting someone else's, and flicked his tail in an incomprehensible gesture. From the corner of her eye, Honey saw the streak of tabby stripes as several dark shapes darted past her and disappeared into the gap. It was the same group of cats that had first surrounded them she realised as she saw Tor follow them. Outside, she suddenly heard a man's voice raised in anger, followed by the yowling of angry cats. *What was going on?*

"It cannot be for long but they will keep him engaged," said Jack. "Enough for you to leave the house unnoticed and take cover."

A rustle sounded in the gap and Tor stuck his grey-striped head back inside. "The man has been drawn away to the other side of the house. But he is no fool, this one. He may yet come back."

"Then you must go now," said Jack, turning back to Honey and the other dogs. "*Senebti*, Big Honey Dog."

He stepped back to allow them through the gap.

Honey felt a rush of gratitude. "Thank you... for everything. If there is ever anything I can do in return..."

The great brown tabby had melted into the shadows again, only his brilliant green and amber eyes showing in the darkness. He said nothing, but Honey felt a promise exchanged, a bond forged. Beyond the opening, she could hear Tor lashing his tail impatiently outside. She took a deep breath and plunged through the gap again.

CHAPTER 21

Outside, the brilliance of the moonlight blinded her for a minute, then she saw Tor slinking away, heading through the overgrown vegetable garden towards a stand of trees beyond. He turned his head and she caught the gleam of his green eyes.

"Hurry!" he hissed.

Honey limped after him and heard the others following behind her. She stumbled through a patch of overgrown pumpkins. Her numb front leg caught on a trailing vine and she tripped, falling to her knees. The other dogs rushed past her.

Ruffster looked back and stopped. "Honey? You all right, mate?"

"Go!" Honey hauled herself painfully to her feet. "I'm right behind you!"

She lunged forwards again, gritting her teeth against the numbing pain in her front leg, trying to drag it with her. It felt even heavier now. She glanced down and recoiled at the sight of her right paw, dark and swollen, with veins running purple up along her leg. That lump squirmed under her skin. She couldn't tear her eyes away from watching it move.

Then a crashing behind her made her jerk her head back. She saw a figure come around the side of the house, that merciless white beam waving in front of it like a predatory antenna. The light dipped, probed, and swooped sideways, catching Honey full in its glare. She blinked, dazzled.

"HONEY!"

"What're you doin'?"

"Don't just stand there! RUN!"

She turned and hobbled blindly in the direction of her friends' voices. More vines tangled under her feet and weeds thrust themselves under her nose. She pushed her way through the long grass, feeling bushes scratch at her sides, leaves slapping in her face. Behind her, she heard the man's voice again and more yowling from the cats. She staggered around a bush and collided into a tree stump. The impact knocked her backwards onto her rump and she sat there, panting, trying to get her bearings.

She had come into the woods—a wide canopy of trees spread over her head, blocking out most of the moonlight. Around her, the bushes crowded thick and dense.

Tor! Her friends! Where were they?

Honey scrambled to her feet and began hobbling in circles, scenting the air urgently. She could pick up their scent, but it seemed to be coming from every direction, mixed with the earthy, moist scents of the forest. She didn't dare bark to call them—in the distance, she could still hear the Dog Catcher's voice and the thrashing sounds as he pushed his way through the undergrowth. The white beam was a faint glow, searching in the distance. Honey hunched her shoulders. She couldn't stay here. He might come this way any moment.

Rustling. Voices. She pricked her ears and turned to the right. Was that Tyson's growl? Did she hear Biscuit's whimper? She started eagerly towards the sound, then stopped, confused. Now the voices seemed to be coming from the left. Then in front of her. Behind her. In the trees above, the wind murmured through the branches, sounding like different voices again. She paced on the spot, panic starting to fill her chest.

Rustling. Behind her.

Honey whirled around. The bushes parted and a black dog stepped out. Not one of her friends, but she thought she recognised him. He must have been following her again but suddenly she didn't care. She was glad to see him. She rushed forwards, her tail wagging.

"Max! How did you get..."

Honey faltered. The moonlight filtering through the leaves caught the gleam of gold and blue stones on his collar and outlined those huge, bat-like ears. It wasn't Max after all. It was that new dog.

"You should not go that way," said Newbie. "He is searching for you."

"Oh, Newbie... what are you doing here?" Honey panted. "Have you seen the others?

I've got to find them... the puppies... I know how to rescue them..."

"The puppiesss?" Newbie said sharply.

"Yes, yes... you must have heard—lots of puppies have gone missing; Bean, too. You know, that Dane pup who was with me... we've been trying to find them." Honey paused to catch her breath. "I know this sounds crazy, but they might have been taken by a... a sort of demon dog from another world..."

Newbie stared at her and made an inarticulate sound in his throat.

"I know," said Honey. "I know it sounds unbelievable, but I think it's true. There have been things that have happened to me too; things that you just wouldn't believe..." Her eyes slid to her front leg and she saw his eyes follow hers, fixing on where her skin was stretched taut over the lump. "Anyway, I've got to get back to the cemetery as soon as possible!" She limped a few steps away, scanning the bushes around them. "Did you see the others?"

"No," said Newbie. "But the man is close."

Honey shuddered. "I've got to avoid him. The feral cats said there's another way back into town—"

"Yesss." Newbie regarded her silently for a moment. "I know the way. Perhapsss you can catch up with your friends. I will show you. Follow me." He turned and trotted off.

Honey stared after him. For a moment something made her hesitate—something that prickled the fur along her back—then she shook herself, sending drool flying in all directions, and started hobbling after him, deeper into the woods.

CHAPTER 22

They pushed their way carefully through the undergrowth with Newbie pausing and listening every so often. Honey pricked her own ears as they paused again; she scented the air and furrowed her brow.

"Are... are you sure this is the right way?" she asked Newbie. "It seems like... We seem to be going *towards* the sounds of the man."

Newbie stopped and tilted his head to the side. "Sounds can be confusing in the woods."

Honey remembered a moment ago when she had thought she could hear voices coming from several directions. He was probably right. She dropped her head and limped after him. Still, she couldn't quite shake off the feeling of unease.

Newbie paused. "Is something wrong?"

"Nooo," said Honey. She gave an embarrassed laugh. "I think all the strange things that have been happening are making me a bit jumpy."

An angry shout from somewhere ahead of them really made her jump. It was the Dog

Catcher and he sounded close.

"Did you hear that?" Honey whispered.

"Yesss," said Newbie.

"Isn't that right in front of us? If we keep going, won't we be walking straight into him?"

Newbie turned and fixed those pale yellow eyes on her. "You do not trusssst me?"

"It's not that...," Honey said hastily, dropping her eyes. Then she froze, staring at his front paws. A picture flashed in her mind of that day in the park when she had first met him and looked down at his paws. Something had struck her as odd then, but she hadn't realised what it was until now.

"Your... your paws... you've only got three toes on each of them," she said slowly, her mind whirling.

"Yesss," Newbie said. "I was born that way." He sat back on his haunches and the moonlight caught his gold collar again. This time it lit the oval disc—that fancy name tag which hung from his collar—illuminating its etched surface. Honey stared, her stomach heaving as she suddenly realised what the etchings were. A leaf, a zigzag line, a square, and a bird with stubby wings. The ancient hieroglyphic language. The pictures which spelled *Inpw*.

She stumbled back from the black dog. "It's... it's you?"

Those pale yellow eyes watched her, unblinking. "It is unfortunate that you had to dissscover my secret. When you told me about the puppiesss and the cemetery, though, I knew it would only be a matter of time."

He moved towards her and Honey scrambled backwards, trying to keep the distance between them. She felt something brush her rump and was surprised to find that it was the rough stone of the cemetery wall. Somehow they had ended up back where the cemetery wall curved through the woods. *Of course, Newbie hasn't been leading me to safety—all this time, he's been leading me towards the Dog Catcher!*

She looked in horror at the dog coming towards her. His eyes—something was wrong with his eyes. They looked unseeing at her, the pupils narrowed to slits, and in their yellow depths was the eerie glow of madness. Then he blinked and the madness was gone. He sat down and gave himself a lazy scratch, for all the world as if they were on a walk in the park.

"Yesss, my name is not 'Newbie' as you dogs all seem to think. It is Nubi, short for *Anubis*." He showed his teeth in a sly smile. "It is one of my many names. I am also known by the name of *Anpu* or—in ancient times—*Inpw*."

Honey just stared. She couldn't think, couldn't take in what he was saying. The hieroglyphic pictures, the stories she heard at the feral cat colony, everything swirled together in her head. "You...you're from *Duat*... from the Underworld...," she said slowly.

Nubi stretched out on the ground and crossed his front paws. "There is a story that tells of when the Firssst Litter was born and all the gods of Old Egypt came to see the pups. There were many pups of different shapes and colours—one with a coat as white as snow, another with fur as red as the sunssset, one with ears like a flowing river, another with legs as long as a gazelle's... and all were coveted by the gods, save one. A small, sickly black pup with neither beautiful eyes nor graceful body. This pup nobody wanted and they would have cassst him out into the dessert for the vultures to feed on... except that the Lord of the Underworld took pity on the pup. He took it back to the shadowy realm of *Duat* where few would have to endure its uglinesss and gave it the job of leading the dead through the Underworld." His yellow eyes flickered. "That pup was me."

Honey swallowed. "I'm sorry."

"Sorry? Why should you be sorry?" Nubi snarled, springing to his feet. "Do you pity me too?"

"No! I mean, yes... er, no... I just meant I felt bad for when you were a puppy. It must have been horrible to be unwanted like that—"

Nubi laughed. The sound made all the hackles on Honey's back stand up. He narrowed his eyes. "Yesss, they did not want me... nobody wanted me... but when they saw how well I served my Massster... *Then*, perhaps, they felt the bite of regret." He curled his muzzle back in a sneer. "What could their pups do? Bark and fawn and wag their tails? I could do so much more." He lowered his voice to a thick whisper. "There is power in the dark realms of *Duat* and I have learnt to use it." His eyes travelled up her swollen front leg to the lump that was now protruding from her shoulder, and he bared his teeth in a sinister smile. "I can show you what I mean."

CHAPTER 23

Honey gasped as a spasm of pain shot through her leg, changing the numbing ice to burning fire. She jerked her head round to look at her shoulder and watched, horrified, as the lump writhed violently under her skin, tugging and stretching until the skin split open, fur and pink flesh peeling away to reveal a pair of black insect mouthparts gnashing and clicking. Scarab. She squealed and reeled backwards, trying to get away, but she couldn't—it was inside her, a part of her, embedded under her skin. She gasped again in pain and dropped to the ground.

Above her, Nubi watched with a smile. "Mm... interesssting... it is different from the puppies."

The puppies? A new wave of horror gripped Honey and gave her the strength to struggle back to her feet. She looked desperately at Nubi. "What do you mean... How... What... *what have you done to the puppies?*"

Nubi turned away and the pain abruptly ceased. The insect mouth stopped moving and the scarab retreated into her flesh again. Cold numbness spread up her leg once more, but Honey was almost grateful. She stood on shaking legs, panting. Dimly she was aware that Nubi was talking again.

"It is a treacherousss journey for the dead to make through the Underworld, and the job of guiding them is not something that can be easily accomplished alone. So I decided that I needed... helpers." He bared his teeth in that sly smile again. "A pack of death hounds who anssswer only to me. But they need to be young—taken from life when it is still uncoloured by experience and their minds are still susceptible to my dominance."

"That's why you told that pet-shop puppy he was too old...," said Honey with sudden understanding. A memory flashed in her mind—the way Nubi's eyes had gleamed when he'd asked how old Bean was and learnt she was only ten weeks old.

"Yesss, sixteen weeks is the end of the window. Even humans know about this time—the firssst sixteen weeks of life—when a puppy's mind is soft and receptive to new things, and all he experiences during this time will determine the dog he will become. It is your one chance to shape his personality— and my chance to bind him to my pack. So it has been for centuries and so has my pack grown."

The Dog Catcher's voice sounded again, close by but muffled by the undergrowth. Honey eyed Nubi in front of her and wondered if there was any way she could get around him, back into the woods beyond. She might be running straight into the Dog Catcher, but she was beginning to think there were worse things to fear than the dog pound.

"I liked you," said Nubi pleasantly. "It is a shame that I have to do this—"

A crashing in the bushes to the right made them both whip their heads around.

Nubi scented the air, then turned his pale yellow eyes back to Honey. "The man comes much fassster than I expected. I will have to let him take care of you for me." He turned and was gone, a shadow merging into the deeper shadows between the trees.

Honey stood for a moment, gaping after Nubi, then the sound of movement in the bushes nearby roused her to action. She couldn't be found here, hemmed in and cut off from all chances of escape. She had to run.

Run.

She threw herself into the undergrowth. Behind her, she heard a bellow of triumph. The Dog Catcher had seen her. His footsteps thundered after her.

She ran. She didn't think; she didn't look back; she just ran. Her front leg dragged uselessly, like one of those rubber chicken toys from the pet shop, but somehow, she still ran. She found herself suddenly back on the trail—the path she had been walking on earlier with the other dogs. This trail led back to the alley behind Max's house. She followed it, gasping and panting. The trail curved round a tree and dipped, and she stumbled, nearly falling over.

Honey stopped and risked a glance backwards. She couldn't see the Dog Catcher. *Have I lost him?* She pricked her ears. Nothing. She turned back and started hobbling again. Soon, ahead of her, she could see where the trail ended and beyond that the opening back into the alley. If she could just make it there, she might have a chance—

"Honey?"

She stopped and looked wildly around. A black dog moved out of the shadows next to her and she recoiled instinctively before she recognised the scarred, muscular body. It was Max.

"Are you OK? Where are the others?" He looked at her in concern.

She panted, trying to catch her breath. "Got... separated... the Dog Catcher—"

Max looked quickly past her. "Is he behind you?"

Honey choked back a gasp. "I... I don't know... think... I've lost him."

Max came up to her and reached out his nose to hers—then he jerked back, his eyes riveted on her shoulder. "*What's that?*"

Honey didn't want to look, but she forced herself to turn her head and look at her shoulder. That gnashing insect mouth was moving again and a thin trickle of blood oozed from the edges of the split skin.

"Is that the thing that was in your leg before?"

Honey nodded numbly.

"Come back to my house with me," said Max. "My Old Man might be able to help—"

A rustling in the bushes beside the trail was all the warning they had. The next minute a figure burst out and loomed above them. It was a man with a long, hard face and cold, grey eyes. He smelled of sour sweat and those smoky white sticks that humans liked to put in their mouths. He held a long pole with a wire noose at one end. The Dog Catcher.

His eyes widened when he saw both of them and a smile lit one corner of his mouth. Honey started backing away, her tail between her legs. Max backed with her, his eyes fixed on the noose. They were only a few metres from the opening into the alley.

"When I say go, turn around and get back into that alley. Run as fast as you can," said Max quietly.

"What about you?"

"I'll be right behind you."

Honey took another step back, then she felt Max bunch his muscles beside her. He snarled suddenly—a ferocious sound—and lunged towards the Dog Catcher. Honey was horrified for a moment, thinking he was going to attack, but he simply snapped at empty air in front of him. The surprise was enough, though, to make the Dog Catcher reel backwards a few steps. It was the distraction they needed.

"Go! GO!" Max yelled.

Honey whirled and bolted for the mouth of the alley. She heard paws scrabbling behind her and knew that Max was following. They were almost there—she had just pushed her

way through the weeds and tall grasses—
when she heard a sharp whine of pain. She
looked over her shoulder, then froze.

Max was thrashing, the wire noose tight
around his neck, cutting deeply into his fur.
The whites of his eyes rolled as he panted
and fought, and his tongue hung out
uselessly. The Dog Catcher was hanging on
grimly, twisting the pole this way and that to
keep Max away from him.

"Max!"

"Don't sto... kee... run..." He gasped.

Honey looked at the alley in front of her,
then back at Max. *I can't just leave him!* She
made her decision, turned back and rushed at
the Dog Catcher, but before she reached him,
something slipped over her neck. And
tightened.

Fear seized her. Honey twisted and jerked.
She heard shouting. Two voices. She yanked
her head back and saw another man standing
behind her, struggling to hold on to the pole
that was attached to the noose around her
neck. He must have come from the alley
behind her. She yelped and pulled, but he
was strong and the noose tightened painfully
around her neck.

Honey stopped finally, gasping for breath,
drool hanging in long white trails from either
side of her mouth. Beside her, Max slumped
down to the ground, his breathing shallow.
He had stopped fighting. They were caught.

CHAPTER 24

The dog pound was not somewhere most pet dogs would ever have visited unless it was in their nightmares. It was a maze of concrete pillars, wire mesh, and metal bars, with bare light bulbs throwing a pale haze over the place. Honey lay on the cold, cement floor of a kennel run, her ears pricking uneasily at the creaks and echoes around her. The place smelled of urine and those strong chemical fumes that sometimes came from the bathroom at home after Olivia had been cleaning. Most of all, it smelled of fear.

She heard movement in the kennel next to hers. The sheet of corrugated iron between them meant she couldn't see through to the other side, but she knew Max was in there. She got up and moved closer to the wall.

"Max?" she whispered. "Are you OK?"

There was a scuffling, then the Pit Bull answered. "Yes. You?"

Honey glanced at her shoulder where a bloody scab was forming around the grotesque insect mouth protruding through her skin. "I'm all right but we need to get out of here. I've got to get back to the cemetery!"

She started pacing back and forth. "The others must have gotten away, but they don't know about Nubi. They don't know he's the one behind the missing puppies... and he might be able to trick them, like he did with me." She shivered, remembering those pale, yellow eyes. "You know, the... the scarabs obey him. He can do things... horrible things. Oh, Max, he hurt me and then he was going to... he was going to..." She broke off, panting with remembered terror.

"But he didn't. You got away from him."

Somehow Max's matter-of-fact statement was more comforting than words of sympathy or reassurance. Honey took a deep breath, pulling herself together.

"Yes," she said more calmly. "Yes, I did." She shook her head. "I can't believe we never suspected him. Ruffster did think he was a bit weird, but I just thought that he was... you know... different. Anyway, the others would never have suspected him, because they were all so convinced it was—" Honey stopped, embarrassed.

"They were all convinced it was me, weren't they? After all, I'm a Pit Bull—I must be evil." Max made a sound like a humourless laugh. "And you? Did you think it was me too?"

Honey shifted uncomfortably, glad Max couldn't see her face. "Well... I did see you with your Old Man carrying that suspicious bundle. And you wouldn't tell me what was in it. But I believed you," she added quickly, "when you said it was nothing to do with the puppies. Even though you wouldn't explain anything. I believed you. And I told the others."

Max's nails clicked on the cement on the other side of the wall. "It's true what I told you—the bundle had nothing to do with the missing puppies." He hesitated. "Although it *was* a puppy. A Pit Bull puppy. My Old Man helps the people who rescued me, and sometimes they find puppies who are being kept by the gangs to be trained as fighting dogs. The people smuggle them out and my Old Man is part of the chain that gets them to safety. But everything has to be kept secret because if the gangs find out—"

"I wouldn't have told!" Honey protested. "Besides, it's not like I can speak to humans anyway."

"I know, I'm sorry." Max paused. "I'm not used to trusting anybody."

Honey sat back, mollified. "Well... I suppose that's good sometimes. If I was more like you, I probably wouldn't have trusted Nubi so much. You knew there was something wrong about him, didn't you? Is that why you attacked him that first day in the park?"

"Yes... In the pit, you learn to read other dogs quickly, to recognise the ones who fight because they have to and the ones who fight because they enjoy hurting others. Nubi had the scent of a killer on him." Max sighed. "But maybe I shouldn't have attacked him. It was exactly what your friends expected from me, wasn't it?"

Honey pawed the ground awkwardly. "I know my friends have said some horrible things to you because... because—"

"Because I'm a Pit Bull."

"Well, yes," Honey admitted. "But you mustn't mind what they say. They don't really mean it."

"Of course they mean it. Everyone means it when it's a Pit Bull."

Honey swallowed. She didn't know what to say. Finally, she said, "Did... did you really fight and kill other dogs?"

There was a long pause. Then Max's voice came, so faint that Honey had to strain her ears to hear him. "Yes. I did. That was a long time ago. In another life. There were men... they beat me with chains... hurt me, made me angry, made me fight...There was blood... so much blood..."

Honey shifted uneasily. One part of her wanted to run away, to stop listening—and another part of her couldn't move.

Max spoke again, his voice distant. "Then one day we were all rescued, taken away from that place. My wounds healed and became scars... and I didn't have to fight anymore. But people still looked at me with fear until my Old Man came. He smiled at me—no one had ever looked at me that way before. It was as if... as if being a Pit Bull didn't matter. And he took me home."

Honey heard Max shake himself, then he said, his voice abrupt, "Why didn't you run?

You could have made it."

"I couldn't just leave you! You could have run yourself, but you distracted the Dog Catcher first so that I would have a better chance. I wasn't going to just abandon you."

There was a long silence from behind the wall.

"No one's ever done something like that for me before." Max's voice was low. "You believed in me too. Even though I couldn't explain about the bundle. You trusted me. "

"Well..." Honey wagged her tail even though she knew Max couldn't see her. "What good is a friend if you can't trust them?"

Max was silent. Then he said quietly, "I've never had a friend before."

Honey touched her nose to the wall between them. "You do now."

A creaking sound made Honey look around. A door opening. She moved to the front of her kennel and peered through the bars. Someone was approaching. It was the Dog Catcher. He came up to Honey's kennel first and started unlocking the door. She backed away, her tail tucked under. He came in and grabbed her collar. Honey jerked away but he was strong. He held her firm while he moved a long box-object over her back. It made a beeping sound and he looked at the box.

"So you gotta microchip... thought you woulda," he muttered. "C'mon—you must be the dog that 'ysterical woman's been calling about."

He clipped a leash on Honey's collar and

started leading her out of the kennel. She braced her feet and resisted, but he gave the leash a sharp yank, forcing her through the kennel door. Outside, she saw Max watching them from his kennel, his nose pressed against the bars.

"Whatcha looking at?" yelled the Dog Catcher. He reached out and kicked the side of Max's kennel. The Pit Bull responded with a deep, guttural growl and the Dog Catcher laughed, an ugly sound.

"Wanna fight, do ya?" He jeered, kicking the side of Max's kennel again.

He tossed Honey's leash through a ring in the wall, picked up a thick, wooden club, and unlocked Max's kennel, stepping inside. Honey's eyes widened in horror. *What was he going to do?*

Max eyed the club. He growled again, deep in his throat, and began backing away.

"C'mon, then!" The Dog Catcher gave his ugly laugh again. "Wanna fight? Huh?"

He thrust forwards, jabbing Max in the side with the club. The Pit Bull whirled around and snarled, but he continued backing away. The Dog Catcher swung the club and jabbed Max on the other side. Then he thrust the club into the Pit Bull's face. Max jerked his head back just in time, snarling and baring his fangs.

"Think yer so tough, huh?" The Dog Catcher grunted, waving the club. "I'll show ya!" He jabbed the club again and again into Max's face, forcing the Pit Bull back into a corner.

Something flared in Max's eyes and he lunged, locking his jaws around the club. The Dog Catcher yanked the club back, dragging Max with him, and kicked the Pit Bull hard in the ribs. Max gave a cry of pain and let go of the club, rolling over on the ground. The Dog Catcher kicked him again. There was a sickening crunch and another whine of pain.

Honey threw herself at Max's kennel, barking furiously, but her leash was tied fast to the wall and all she did was choke herself as it yanked tight.

"Hello?"

They all turned. A woman stood in the far doorway, peering in. Honey recognised the Pet Sitter. She saw Honey at the same time and rushed forwards.

"Oh, thank God, you've found her! I was so worried... I didn't know what I was going to tell her owner. Oh, Honey! Where have you been all day?" She unclipped Honey's collar from the leash attached to the wall and threw her arms around Honey's neck, squeezing hard. "You naughty dog! How could you run off like that?" She looked up hopefully. "Did you find my puppy too? Bean? I reported her missing—she's a Dane too. She's only about ten weeks old—"

"No, ma'am." The Dog Catcher lowered his club and stepped out of Max's kennel. "No sign of 'er or any t'other missing pups."

"Oh, please let me know as soon as you have any news," the Pet Sitter pleaded. "I don't understand how she could have just disappeared like that... I only took my eyes off her for a second!"

"Them dog thieves can be pretty smart." The Dog Catcher took out a white stick and stuck it in his mouth. "Betcha some gang's stealing pups fer fighting."

"Fighting?" The Pet Sitter looked shocked.

The Dog Catcher shrugged and gestured to Max's kennel. "Like this Pit Bull 'ere... killer fighting dog, 'e is."

"Him?" The girl looked over Honey's shoulder at Max in his kennel. The Pit Bull was struggling to stand, panting heavily, froth gathering at the corners of his mouth. "But... but he looks... Are you sure? He looks like someone's pet... that collar and name tag—"

"Oh, yeah. Some sucka been to some rescue that got 'im outta some fighting ring and tried to turn 'im into a pet. Pah!" The Dog Catcher spat. "You dunno dogs like I do, ma'am. Them Pit Bulls can't be trusted— attack you fer no reason. Went into 'is kennel to be friendly just now and 'e just went for me! Tried to take a chunk outta me. Vicious brute."

Honey stared at the Dog Catcher in disbelief. *How could he tell such lies?*

"He sounds dangerous." The Pet Sitter gave Max a scared look. "What are you going to do?"

"Don'cha worry." The Dog Catcher sucked on the white stick, then blew some smoke into the air. "Gonna make sure I teach 'im a lesson 'e won't forget." He smiled and held the club up, then stepped back into Max's kennel.

NO! Not again! Honey reared up like a horse and lunged forwards, yanking herself out of the Pet Sitter's arms. There was a shriek as the woman lost her balance and fell over backwards. Honey charged into Max's kennel and threw herself at the Dog Catcher, pounding her front paws on his chest. She knocked him over and fell on top of him. One of his arms shoved hard against her numbed right shoulder, right where the scarab was under her skin.

Something moved inside her shoulder.

The Dog Catcher screamed and jerked away from her, his eyes suddenly scared. He looked down at his arm where it had been pressed against her shoulder, and his face contorted in pain. He pressed the other hand over his arm and blood oozed out from between his fingers.

Honey staggered backwards, not understanding what had happened. She hadn't bitten him. So where had the blood come from? Then she felt something move in her shoulder again and looked down. That mouth—that hideous scarab mouth—was chewing, chewing, chewing, and in its bloody jaws was what looked like a scrap of human flesh.

"Oh my Dog," she whispered, feeling sick. "It bit him. The scarab bit him and now it...it's eating—"

"Honey!" Max was next to her. "Come on! Now's our chance!"

The Pit Bull darted out of the kennel, and after a dazed moment, Honey followed him.

They shot past the Pet Sitter who was still groaning on the ground and bolted towards the open doorway and freedom.

CHAPTER 25

The journey across town was harrowing as they crept through the dark streets, constantly looking over their shoulders. Honey was having trouble dragging her numb front leg and she could hear Max's laboured breathing next to her. In the glow of a passing streetlight, she could see his eyes glazed with pain and a thin trickle of blood oozing from the side of his mouth. She remembered his cry of pain and that horrible crunching sound when the Dog Catcher had kicked him, and she didn't want to think about what might be wrong with him.

The moon was high now and it was nearly midnight. As they turned into Lemon Tree Lane, they could clearly see the tall iron gates of the cemetery, open and waiting at the bottom. Honey slowed as they approached the gates and looked towards Max's house, then at the panting Pit Bull beside her.

"You don't have to come," she said urgently. "You're hurt. You should go back home and get your Old Man to take you to the vet."

Max shook his head, his body hunched over in pain.

Honey shifted her paws. "But—"

A sudden flurry of movement out of the corner of her eye made her look up. It was the other dogs, spilling out of the narrow passageway between Max's house and the cemetery wall. Their eyes brightened as they saw Honey and they rushed forwards, only to pause uncertainly as they saw Max as well. Honey went forwards to meet them.

"Honey! You're OK!"

"We were so worried!"

"Yeah, mate, we were searchin' all over for you—then we figured we'd come here and wait for—"

"What's *he* doing here?" growled Tyson, eyeing the Pit Bull.

"Max saved me," said Honey. "I wouldn't be here if it wasn't for him." Quickly, she told them what had happened. Suka's blue eyes nearly popped out of her head.

"It's been Nubi all along," said Honey. "Max had nothing to do with it."

The others looked over at the Pit Bull. Suka still looked disbelieving whilst Tyson looked like he had eaten something too big that he couldn't quite swallow. Biscuit raised his nose in Max's direction and sniffed cautiously.

Ruffster scratched his ear, looking slightly puzzled. "You really like him, don't you?"

Honey lifted her muzzle. "He's my friend. Just like you—and Biscuit and Suka and

Tyson."

"Well, it's just... him bein' Pit Bull and all—"

"He's a dog," said Honey firmly. "Just like any of us."

Ruffster scratched his ear again and looked at the ground. "Yeah... I guess."

Tyson gave a snort and turned away, walking into the cemetery with his tail stiff. Suka and Biscuit followed. Honey waited while Max walked slowly over to join them.

"Er... paws up, mate," said Ruffster, reaching out gingerly to sniff Max's bum.

The Pit Bull stood silently as Ruffster circled him. He was still breathing heavily and his eyes were dull with pain. Honey opened her mouth again to suggest that he go home, but Max cut her off.

"I'm coming with you," he said. "I just need a moment." Max lay down heavily and Honey sat next to him, glad of the chance to take her weight off her front leg.

Ruffster paced around them, looking like he wanted to speak to Max, but unsure about what to say. Finally, he looked through the cemetery gates and said awkwardly: "Er... reckon I'd better go tell the others what's happenin', otherwise they'll wonder where we are." He hurried off without waiting for an answer.

Max watched him go. "They're scared of me."

"For kibble's sake, don't let Tyson hear you say that!" said Honey with a small laugh. "He's a bit sensitive about stuff like that and... *er*... about his size." She hesitated. "I...I know Tyson comes across a bit cranky sometimes, but he's not a bad dog, you know. Once he's your friend, he'll do anything for you. The others too. They just need a bit of time."

Max gave her a long look but didn't say anything. He heaved himself to his feet and they made their way into the cemetery, heading towards the area where the pet memorials were. Honey could see the other dogs gathered around that strange memorial stone that was set apart from the others. Beyond it was the fresh mound of earth, raked back and disturbed from where they had been digging last time. She couldn't stop her eyes darting around, half expecting black scarabs to erupt out of the ground around them at any moment. But today, all seemed quiet. Eerily quiet.

As she got closer, she saw that the other dogs had actually been digging, pushing aside more of the fresh earth to reveal what was buried underneath. Deeper than where the pile of puppy collars had been, she could see a big, rectangular slab of stone emerging from the ground. Suka was down on the stone and the Husky swept her plumed tail across the surface, brushing the last of the loose earth away.

There were deep rectangular lines cut into the stone slab and its whole surface was covered in pictures. Little pictures just like those in Suka's Boy's book. More hieroglyphics. They marched up and down and across the slab. Several formed a row that followed the deep grooves cut into the stone—up one side of the slab, across the top, and down the other side again, framing what looked like a doorway. Honey caught her breath. It *was* a door. A door lying on the ground. A door to the Underworld.

"Reckon it's one of those *Ka* doors the ferals were talkin' about?" asked Ruffster in a hushed voice.

"How do we open it?" asked Suka eagerly.

Biscuit thrust his nose against the stone slab, his whiskers quivering. "The puppies' scent—I can smell it. They've been through here recently."

Honey scrambled down next to Suka and sniffed along the deep rectangular grooves in the slab. She pawed at it. She pushed. Nothing moved. Tyson jumped down as well and started trying to dig along the groove. They all watched hopefully—there was almost nothing that Tyson couldn't dig through—but after a minute, he growled in frustration and stepped back.

"Solid stone," he said in disgust.

"Maybe it needs a key?" suggested Biscuit. "You know, like our doors at home—"

"Don't reckon this door is anythin' like our doors at home," said Ruffster, walking around it.

"Hey! Look, there's a bigger picture in the middle," Suka said, cocking her head.

The others followed her gaze. She was right. In the centre of the slab—right in the middle of where the doorway would be—was a larger drawing. It showed a black dog with yellow eyes and huge, bat-like ears standing next to what looked like a giant scale. The two plates of the scale were balanced and on the left plate was a heart, on the right plate, a feather.

On the other side of the scale in the drawing was a grotesque creature—Honey had never seen anything like it before. It looked like somebody had put lots of animals in a bowl and mixed them together so that different parts got stuck together. Whatever it was, she didn't like the look of those rows of sharp teeth or that long, creepy tail.

"That black dog in the picture sure looks like Nubi," commented Suka.

"It *is* Nubi," Honey said, her eyes riveted on the drawing. "This must be his personal dog door that leads to the realms of *Duat*. And our way in to rescue the puppies."

CHAPTER 26

Biscuit walked up and down the stone slab of the *Ka* door, sniffing along the surface. "What about all these little pictures? They're hieroglyphics, aren't they? They're just like the ones on the memorial stone." He paused at four specific pictures. "Look, Honey, this set is just like the one you remembered."

"Yes, the one that spells *Inpw*," said Honey, her eyes widening.

"There was a curse written on the memorial stone," said Biscuit, sniffing worriedly. "Maybe there's a curse written on this too."

"Or..." Ruffster stopped pacing, his eyes excited. "Or maybe not a curse... maybe they're givin' instructions on how to open this door!"

Suka flicked her fluffy tail. "But how can we work it out? I haven't got my Boy's book here and I don't remember what all the pictures mean—"

"Wait!" Honey turned excitedly to Biscuit. "Biscuit! You ate that page, didn't you? The one with the chart of all the little pictures."

The Beagle looked embarrassed and cast a furtive look at Suka. "It was an accident, OK?"

"Can you regurgitate it?" Honey asked.

"I suppose... I can try," said Biscuit reluctantly. He hunched over and began making retching sounds. *"Gru-gru-gruugh!"* Biscuit opened his mouth and spat out several objects. A partially digested pig ear, a lipstick, half a sandwich, a golf ball, three pieces of soggy kibble—and there, amongst the gooey mess, was a crumpled piece of paper.

Suka made a face as she pulled it out. "My Boy's page! Look what you've done to it!"

Everybody leaned in to peer at the piece of paper. Max started forwards but stopped as Tyson and Suka moved closer, blocking him out of the circle with their shoulders. Honey's heart sank. Then she saw Ruffster shift aside to make room for Max, giving the Pit Bull an awkward wag of his tail. Smiling to herself, Honey turned back to the soggy page. The figures were a bit wet and blurry, but it was still possible to match them up to the pictures on the stone slab.

"There are so many, though!" Suka said in dismay, looking across the surface of the slab. "Where should I start? We could be here all night deciphering them."

"Do the ones around the doorway first," said Honey. "They should be the most important."

They watched in impatient silence as Suka

slowly matched the pictures engraved on the stone slab to the ones on the chart and decoded the message.

"*Enter... enter those... enter those who tread with balance,*" murmured Suka.

"*Enter those who tread with balance?*" Ruffster repeated. "What's that supposed to mean? It's not another o' those stupid riddles, is it?"

"It's telling ya how to get in," growled Tyson. "If ya *tread with balance*, then ya can enter."

"Tread sort of means to step on something," said Suka thoughtfully. "It was on my Boy's vocabulary list last term."

"So we have to step somewhere on the door?" asked Ruffster, jumping onto the slab and bouncing around. "Nothin's happenin'."

"Maybe you have to step somewhere special," suggested Biscuit. "My Missus keeps my kibble in this big plastic bin in the kitchen and I found out that if you push your paw on a part of the cover, the lid will spring open. But only if you hit that exact spot where there's a sort of raised bump." He grinned and wagged his tail. "She doesn't know I've figured that out yet."

"That big picture," said Honey, looking again at the engraving of Nubi next to the scales. "I'm sure the special spot is somewhere on that big picture."

"The scales!" cried Ruffster, rushing over to the picture and planting himself on top of the plate on one side of the scale. Biscuit hurried to the other plate and sat on that.

They waited expectantly. Nothing happened. Biscuit whined in disappointment and Ruffster's ears drooped.

"You have to be balanced." Max spoke up for the first time. "You're different sizes. I think it will work if you have dogs of the same size on both sides of the scale."

The dogs all looked up in surprise. Max had been so quiet that they had almost forgotten he was there. Suka's blue eyes brightened with interest and Ruffster perked up. Even Tyson looked impressed by Max's suggestion.

"Yes!" said Honey excitedly. "Quick—how much do you all weigh?"

"Eight kilos," growled Tyson.

"I'm twenty-four kilos," said Suka and looked at Ruffster. "What about you?"

"Sixteen, mate" said Ruffster. "And don't bother askin' Honey—none o' us could balance her out."

Honey ducked her head self-consciously. "Yes, I'm about seventy kilos." She looked at Max enquiringly.

The Pit Bull hesitated, then said, "I'm about thirty."

They all turned to Biscuit. He squirmed. "Do I have to? Oh, all right... I'm about fourteen kilos. But I think some of that's my collar! It's a really heavy one!"

Honey sighed. "Well, that's no good. We're all different sizes. How are we going to balance the scales?"

"Maybe... maybe two dogs can stand on one side together," said Suka slowly.

"Ruffster—you're sixteen kilos, right? And I'm twenty-four... so you just need another eight kilos to make you the same weight as me!"

"That's me!" growled Tyson, stepping onto the plate next to Ruffster.

Biscuit moved off the other side of the scales and Suka took his place. Now there were twenty-four kilos on both sides of the scale. They all waited with bated breath. For a moment nothing happened, then a deep rumbling sounded in the ground beneath them. The stone slab began to vibrate, sending loose earth from the mound around it raining down on the dogs.

"Holy liver treat!" said Ruffster, struggling to stay in place.

With a creaking groan, the section in the middle of the slab began to shift and move. The dogs barely had time to jump aside before the grooves marking the doorway deepened, and then the entire middle section of the slab swung inwards.

A doorway yawned in the ground, with steps leading down into the darkness. A doorway into the Underworld.

CHAPTER 27

The steps led down to a tunnel. The dogs went as quickly as they dared, eyes straining to see ahead of them, noses twitching for any scent. The floor of the tunnel was covered with sand—a soft, yellow stuff, almost like powder—which shifted treacherously beneath their paws with each step. Flaming logs were stuck in holders along the walls of the tunnel. They gave off a dim, flickering orange glow, throwing eerie shadows against the walls and sending small fingers of light into the tunnel ahead.

The walls themselves were covered with engravings—rows upon rows of hieroglyphics and pictures of other things: strange birds with hooked beaks, spotted cows and writhing snakes; trees with branches that sprouted like feathers, and many, many humans with black hair and white robes, all standing facing sideways. And all with eyes that seemed to move and follow the dogs as they walked past. Honey felt her hackles stand rigid along her back. She kept her own eyes forwards, trying not to look at the pictures.

Biscuit was ahead, his nose along the ground, snuffling through the sand. As they came to a curve in the tunnel, he paused, sniffing the air intently.

"What is it?" whispered Honey. "Is something around the corner?"

The Beagle shook his head as if trying to clear something from his ears. "I don't know... I thought..."

Honey took a deep sniff. She could smell the smoke from the flaming logs, and beneath that the air smelt dead and empty, like a room that had been forgotten and hadn't been opened for a long time. She took a deep breath and stepped around the corner. Something crunched under her paw. She glanced down. For a moment, she thought it was dead leaves, but she knew there were no dead leaves underground. Besides, it was something harder. Something black. Her heart lurched. She bent down to sniff it.

"Holy liver treat," Ruffster whispered next to her, his eyes wide. "Don't tell me that's a...?"

"Scarab," confirmed Honey. "But it's dead." She looked around, her eyes adjusting to the dim light. "There're lots of them. Everywhere."

Everyone froze, eyes darting around, ears straining for the *click-click-click* of that seething black army. But all was silent.

After a moment, Honey said, "I don't think they're here. Maybe these are just some dead bugs left behind."

She limped forwards again, although she did pick her paws up higher in an effort to avoid stepping on the dead scarabs. The other dogs did the same as they continued down the tunnel's winding route. Soon they noticed the tunnel widening and the ceiling arching higher above their heads. Honey felt something tickle her whiskers—a draught of cold air that suggested a wider, more open space ahead. Then she heard a sound that she couldn't quite believe. A rushing, gurgling, splashing sound.

Ruffster cocked his upright ear. "Is that...?"

"Water." Suka nodded, her blue eyes bright with anticipation. "It sounds like an underground river!"

They quickened their steps. Honey found herself falling behind the others as her numb front leg dragged uselessly against the ground. She hobbled sideways to avoid stepping on another dead scarab. And then she saw it.

It lay there, half-buried in the sand: Bean's pink-and-purple collar.

She gasped and pounced on it, ignoring the burning pain in her shoulder. The others stopped and looked back.

Biscuit hurried back to sniff the collar. "Her scent's fresh!" he said, wagging his tail. "She's been through here recently."

She's here! Honey felt a surge of hope and happiness that for a moment blotted out all the numbing pain. "Bean!" she yelped, pushing past the others to hobble ahead. "BEAN!"

"Wait, Honey!" Suka hissed, chasing after her, the other dogs at her heels. "You don't know what's—"

She broke off as they rounded the last bend in the tunnel and entered a vast hall. The ceiling soared above their heads into darkness, and the edges of the hall disappeared into purple gloom so that it was impossible to see where the hall began and where it ended. In fact, it no longer felt like they were underground but somewhere else entirely. Somewhere In-Between.

Massive stone pillars rose out of the floor of the hall, their sides etched with more hieroglyphics. Between the pillars were many statues, but Honey's eyes were drawn to the huge one of a black dog lying on its haunches, its bat-like ears erect, its yellow-jewel eyes glittering. And next to this statue stood something that looked familiar—a tall golden column with a bar across the top and two plates dangling from gold chains at either end of the bar. *A scale!* Honey recognised it as a giant version of the scale from the picture outside on the stone *Ka* door.

"I was right about the river," whispered Suka next to her.

Stretching across the hall was a river of roiling black water. It emerged from the back of the hall, flowed swirling and ebbing past them to the other end of the vast chamber and then seemed to stop and fall over the edge into an abyss. Mist rose from the black emptiness beyond the edge of the waterfall, but they could not hear water crashing below. Just the sound of water rushing, sighing, falling into emptiness.

Then Honey saw something that made her forget everything else: the boat on the river. It was a shallow wooden craft tied to a post on the bank. The thin rope that secured it was stretched taut by the water rushing under the boat, trying to pull it free.

The boat was filled with puppies.

And on the bank next to the boat stood Nubi. He looked up as they entered, and between his front paws, they saw a tiny, white puppy. She looked about eight weeks old and lay flopped on her side. She might have been sleeping, except that she was lying unnaturally still and her eyes were open but vacant. *They're all like that*, Honey realised, scanning the huddle in the boat. There was no bouncing, no squealing, no tumbling or playing that you'd expect from a group of puppies that age. Instead, they all lay still and silent, their eyes blank, their mouths sagging.

"Oh my Dog, what has he done to the puppies?" whispered Biscuit.

Something black scuttled between two of the puppy bodies and Honey recoiled in horror. There were scarabs crawling all over the puppies and each puppy had a black beetle latched on to one of its paws, the scarab's mouthparts digging into the puppy's skin, sucking and pumping.

"The scarabs!" Ruffster stared, transfixed.

"It's like the one in your leg, Honey—they're bitin' the pups and usin' their creepy insect drool to paralyse them!"

"We've got to get those bugs off them," said Suka, her eyes wide.

Honey took a step forwards, then her heart lurched as she saw one bundle that was much bigger than the others, with huge puppy paws tucked against a soft, round belly.

"Bean!" she cried, rushing forwards.

"*Keep back!*" snarled Nubi, baring his fangs.

The echo of his snarl seemed to surge around the hall and writhe around them like a snake of cold air hissing at their shoulders. Honey stood her ground and pulled back her own jowls in a ferocious snarl. Great Danes might be known as big softies, but the blood of ancient boarhounds still coursed in their veins. When needed, they could be fierce defenders.

Nubi laughed—a sinister sound that echoed around the hall. "Foolish dog! Do you think you are any match for me?" He turned his pale yellow eyes on the others as they moved to join Honey. "It is too late anyway. The puppies are ready for their final journey."

He picked up the white pup by its scruff and tossed it into the boat with the others. "A snap of this rope and they will be gone. Over the waterfall and into the abysss... down to the realms of *Duat*. And there is nothing you can do. Entry into *Duat* is forbidden for the living."

"There are seven o' us, mate, and only one o' you," said Ruffster, baring his own teeth.

Nubi laughed again. He stepped forwards and pulled his ears back, opening his mouth wide until it seemed to yawn like the dislocated jaws of a snake. From the depths of his throat came a hissing, guttural call:

"Asswad ju… yuhattim khassim!"

Then he shook himself violently—starting from the tips of his huge, bat-like ears and moving down along his sleek, black body to the end of his curling tail—like a wet dog trying to shake himself dry. But it was not water droplets that came flying out from his fur. Instead, tiny black flecks burst from his body, raining in black showers to the ground all around him.

"Euugh," said Ruffster, taking a step back. "That is a serious flea problem."

"Those aren't fleas…," growled Tyson, his hackles bristling.

He was right, Honey realised with a cold, sick feeling in her stomach as she watched the tiny black specks swell and grow, each expanding into a shiny black beetle. The air filled with the sound of sinister *click-clicking* as a thousand scarabs surged forwards and surrounded them.

CHAPTER 28

The dogs backed away, trying to move towards the tunnel, but the scarabs fanned around them, encircling them in a seething black mass of gnashing mandibles and bristling legs. There was no escape now. Honey and her friends edged closer together, rump to rump, facing outwards in a circle.

"Er... I hate to say this, but I'm gettin' a bad sense of déjà vu," muttered Ruffster.

"Honey! Can't you do that thing with your drool again?" asked Biscuit, scooting backwards and pressing against her, his eyes fixed on the scarabs.

Honey swallowed and licked her jowls, realising with a small shock that for the first time in her life, she wasn't drooling. Her mouth was dry with fear and her tongue felt like a strip of rawhide that had been left to shrivel in the sun. "I can't."

The scarabs surged forwards another inch, and Honey gasped suddenly as pain shot through her shoulder. Something squirmed violently under her skin. She looked down to where the skin had split open to reveal that hideous black insect mouth. Except that now it wasn't just the mouth she could see but the whole head of a scarab beetle. It twisted and squirmed, its jaws working. Blood oozed from the torn skin around it. She staggered and dropped to her knees, panting.

"Honey!"

"Honey—are you OK?"

Honey felt several wet noses press against her. Max stepped in front of her, shielding her from the scarabs with his body. Honey took a deep breath and struggled back to her feet, gritting her teeth against the pain that was burning in her shoulder. Around them, the circle shrank as the beetles inched closer.

Suka stared at them, wild-eyed. "What are we going to do?"

"We could take them" growled Tyson. "If we all attack together—"

"There are too many," said Max. "You might survive one scarab inside you—like Honey—but more than that and they'll eat you alive."

"Have ya got a better idea?" snapped Tyson.

Honey looked desperately at the black army of beetles crawling around them, then at the puppies still in the boat. They couldn't win this. Not by fighting.

"Wait!" Honey yelled. "Nubi, wait!"

The black dog turned his pale yellow eyes on her. The scarabs stopped moving forwards.

"Tell me why," said Honey. "You never said why you're doing this."

"Why?" Nubi repeated, baring his fangs in a slow smile.

"Honey—what are you doin'?" hissed Ruffster incredulously. "Psycho Demon Dog is tryin' to kill us here and you think he needs to see a behaviourist?"

Honey ignored him and looked at Nubi again. "You said that puppies have been joining your pack of death hounds for centuries... but those are all puppies who died and entered the Underworld already. You've never come and taken living puppies from our world before, have you?"

"No," growled Nubi. "There has been no need before—otherwise I would not have had to come and live amongssst you, abasing myself like a pet dog!" He wrinkled his muzzle in disgust. "Aggression, disease, famine, danger—they have long provided me with a rich and continual puppy harvessst. But the world is changing. The interference of Man with his vaccinations, his medicines, his food, and his pampering has robbed me of the puppy lives I could have taken." His yellow eyes gleamed. "But now I wait no longer. What violence and disease will not provide me, I will take myself."

"But why?" insisted Honey. "Why do you need to do that? Did your Master tell you to come and steal puppies?"

"No," spat Nubi. "The Massster knows nothing of this."

"Then what happens if he finds out?" asked Honey.

Nubi shifted, looking unsure for the first

time. "No...," he muttered. "Massster has said nothing taken from the living, but this is different—"

"But what if he doesn't think so?" Honey said. "My human—*er*, my master—is really strict about the rules, no exceptions. I would get into big trouble if I disobeyed her. She can get really angry..." Honey paused and looked squarely into those pale yellow eyes. "What if *your* Master gets angry... angry enough to throw you out into the desert again?"

Nubi blanched and for a moment, Honey saw the scared, unwanted puppy that he once was.

"He would not do that!" he snarled, but those pale yellow eyes looked scared and uncertain.

"Are you *sure*?" Honey said. "If he finds out, how are you going to explain it to him? If your Master is really angry at what you've done... Do you want to be abandoned and unwanted again?"

Nubi howled in frustration, but Honey could see he was really hesitating now. Around them, the black beetle army began to retreat, fading back into the shadows, their *clicks* stuttering into silence. Across in the boat, the scarabs released the puppies and crawled off their bodies.

Honey felt a sharp tugging in the muscles of her shoulder, then with a squelch like a boil bursting, the black scarab squeezed out from under her skin and fell to the ground. Blood oozed down her leg in a thick, dark stream, but the numbing pain lessened. The scarab scuttled off into the shadows to join its own kind. Honey sighed with relief as all her muscles seemed to loosen and relax. She wriggled her toes. They tingled, but more like the tingle you get after you've woken up in a funny position and your legs have gone to sleep. It was a nasty prickling sensation, but Honey was glad just to be able to feel it.

She looked back up at Nubi. He was still looking angry and undecided. Then he brightened. "There is a way to end this!" he said, looking suddenly across the hall. The dogs followed his gaze to the huge golden scale. "A tessst. From my Massster."

Nubi walked slowly across the hall to the scale. Honey hesitated, glancing back at the puppies in the boat, then turned to follow Nubi. The others fell into step beside her. They watched as the black dog circled the scale.

"All those who come through here mussst passs the Weighing of the Heart... their hearts weighed againssst the Feather of *Ma'at*."

Nubi leaned towards the right plate of the scale and breathed onto its surface. A puff of vapour issued from his mouth, like your breath on a cold day, and when it cleared, a large ostrich feather was resting on the plate. The scale dipped slightly to the right.

"If they pass the tessst—if their hearts are lighter than the Feather—then they are free. But if their lives have been filled with evil deeds—deeds that weigh down their hearts— then they will be devoured."

"Devoured?" said Ruffster, under his breath. "Gettin' a bit melodramatic, isn't he?"

A deep swishing in the river made them all jerk their heads around. Something was moving in the black water. Biscuit raised his nose towards the river, then began whimpering.

"What? Biscuit, what is it?" Suka demanded.

The Beagle began backing away from the river, still whimpering. "Th...the smell of death!"

Honey and the others stared at the water. A pair of eyes broke the surface—empty, opaque, reptile eyes. The eyes were followed by a long scaly snout with hooked teeth protruding from uneven jaws. But where the neck of the reptile should have been was a thick mane of black and yellow hair, and behind that came massive, muscular shoulders that moved with a feline grace. Then the body changed again, bowing into short, squat legs covered in a leathery grey skin. The creature rose from the river, black water streaming from its body, and lashed a giant, scaly tail topped with a row of hard ridges.

Honey caught her breath. It was the grotesque creature from that picture on the *Ka* door outside, brought to life—the lethal jaws and head of a crocodile merging into the massive shoulders and front paws of a lion and finishing in the powerful rear of a hippopotamus with a long, scaly tail.

The dogs edged away from the river as the

creature crawled out onto the bank and made its slow way over to Nubi.

"Meet *Ammut*—Devourer of the Dead," said Nubi, baring his teeth in another slow smile. "Like us dogs, she is always hungry."

Ammut opened her jaws and a foul stench spewed out—the smell of vomit, of rotting fish, of a raw bone that had been left out in the garden for too long. The dogs reeled back and gagged.

Nubi seemed unbothered by the stench. He glanced towards the puppies in the boat and said: "The Weighing of the Heart shall decide if the puppiesss stay with me or are... released. My Massster cannot be angry with this—the tessst follows his decree. But..." He looked back at them. "Since the puppiesss have not yet lived their lives, they cannot take the tessst themselves. So I will let one of you take their place."

"One of us?" said Ruffster with a gulp.

"Yesss," said Nubi, "but choose wisely. For whoever steps forwards mussst be very sure that his good deeds outweigh his bad. If you fail the tessst... you will have to fight Ammut for your own life. And the lives of the puppies."

"F...fight that?" Ruffster said hoarsely, looking over at the creature.

Nubi narrowed his yellow eyes. "Yesss and beware: Ammut is born of a crocodile, a lion, and a hippopotamusss—each more than a match for any dog on its own—but in her, you will be facing them with their strengths combined."

A tense silence fell over the hall. Then one of the dogs stepped forwards.

"I'll do it," said Max the Pit Bull.

CHAPTER 29

"What?" Honey turned around to stare at Max. "No, Max—no! You can't!"

The other dogs stared at Max too, surprise in their eyes—and something else. Something that had never been there before. Something like respect.

Honey whined urgently. "Max, you can't! You know you can't! We've all done bad things but you... It's different for you." She moved to block his way as the Pit Bull started forwards. "You're crazy! You know with your dogfighting past... your chances of passing the test—"

Max paused and looked across at the puppies in the boat, then back at Honey. "I cannot change my past. The things I've done—the things I was forced to do—still fill my sleep with nightmares. But I can choose my own future." His voice dropped. "And the bloodstains on my paws... maybe I'll finally be able to lick them away."

"No, no... I'll do it!" said Honey. "I...I'm the biggest dog here, right? So even if I fail the test, I'd have a much better chance against the monster—"

"Fighting is not just about size," Max said. "Saving the pups depends on you winning that fight... and even if you knew how, you're in no condition to fight." He looked pointedly at Honey's bleeding shoulder.

"Neither are you," said Honey quickly. "You've been hurt too. The way that Dog Catcher kicked you... You don't know what's been injured inside and—"

"I'm used to fighting with injuries," said Max quietly. "Those dark days in the pit... being thrown back inside with wounds still fresh from the last fight... If nothing else, those years of pain and torture have at least prepared me for this." He raised his head. "Let me do this. This is one fight I will walk into with my head high."

Shouldering her gently aside, he stepped forwards towards Nubi and the huge, golden scale. The other dogs moved back to let him pass, and for the first time, they looked him properly in the eyes. Suka gave her fluffy tail a small, encouraging wag while Biscuit let out a soft "*A-woo-woo-woo*".

Ruffster reached out tentatively with his nose. "*Er*... best o' luck, mate."

Max dipped his head, then locked his eyes with Tyson's.

The Jack Russell returned his look and gave a low growl. "Good luck."

Max dipped his head again. He turned back and looked at Honey. She forced her tail out from under her belly and tried to give him a brave wag. His eyes softened, then he turned and stepped up to the scales.

"Breathe on the plate," instructed Nubi, standing beside the empty plate on the left side of the scale. On the other side, the ghostly Feather of *Ma'at* rested on the right plate.

Max took a deep breath and exhaled softly. Misty vapour swirled from his jaws and collected on the left plate, coiling to form the shape of a heart. There was a creak and jingle of chains as the bar of the scale began to move, the two sides rising and dipping like a see-saw. The dogs stared, transfixed. Honey felt her breath fluttering in her throat.

The bar rocked slower and slower.

Left. Right. Left. Right.

Left. Right.

Left... Right...

Left...

Right...

Left.......

It stopped.

The plate on the left side dipped down.

"You have failed the tessst!" hissed Nubi, his eyes gleaming.

Behind him came a roar that shook the hall and Ammut loomed out of the shadows, her blank, dead eyes fixed on Max. She came forwards, long tail curving through the sand, her jaws swinging open, letting another wave of foul stench fill the air.

Honey saw Max's eyes darting around Ammut's body, searching for the creature's vulnerable spots, and she felt her stomach twist in panic as she followed his gaze. *How was Max going to fight her?* The reptile scales that covered Ammut's head and snout were impenetrable to a dog's teeth, and her thick lion's mane protected the soft underside of her throat. The back part of her body that was hippo was covered in slippery, leathery skin that would be hard to get a grip on, and that long lashing tail was enveloped again by the hard scales. The only vulnerable parts of Ammut were her furry belly, chest, and shoulders, but to reach them, Max would have to get past those deadly teeth and slashing claws.

"Festerin' fleas—he's never goin' to have a chance," muttered Ruffster beside her.

"But he was a champion fighter, wasn't he?" argued Suka. "He probably thinks he can take her on."

No, Honey thought. Max must have known. He must have known what his chances were. Just like with the Weighing of the Heart. And yet still he had stepped forwards.

Max lowered his head. The muscles rippled across his shoulders as he began pacing sideways, his steps measured, keeping Ammut in front of him. He thrust his muzzle out and snarled.

The fight was on.

They circled, eyes on each other, muscles tensed to strike. Then Ammut lunged, those crocodile jaws snapping with deadly precision. But Max was faster. He dodged, twisted, and veered back, his teeth ripping into the monster's shoulder. Ammut roared and swung around, slamming into Max with the side of her head and knocking him to the ground. But the Pit Bull was up again in a flash, paws braced in the sand, circling.

Honey had only seen Max in action once before—the time Tyson had forced him into a fight—and then he had been holding himself back. There was none of that now. She barely recognised the dog before her—his eyes hard and focused with deadly intent, the muscles taut in that scarred body, the veins bulging in his legs.

Ammut whirled and swiped a front paw, talons flashing. Max jumped back, barely missing the razor-sharp lion's claws. Ammut roared and lunged again just as Max launched himself forwards, and they collided in the middle. Honey backed away from the maelstrom in front of her. They were a blur of snapping jaws and flying fur, raking claws and lashing tail. Max rearing up on his hind legs. Ammut flipping over. Bodies slamming together and rolling apart. Blood dripping and smearing across the sand. The sound of teeth clashing and claws scraping the ground.

Then they fell back from each other, circling again.

Honey released the breath she had been holding as Ruffster and the others began barking excitedly. They were cheering, she realised as she looked at Ammut and saw that there were bite marks on the monster's skin in several places. Her mane was ragged now and teeth had been broken from her gaping jaws.

Honey felt a surge of hope, then her heart lurched as she looked at Max. The Pit Bull was panting heavily, foam lining his mouth. He was bleeding from several places, and one of his back legs dragged uselessly in the sand. Along his body, three parallel, bloody lines could be seen where one of Ammut's talons had raked down his back. But it was the look in his eyes that scared Honey. They were feverishly bright with pain.

Next to her, Tyson muttered something and made a compulsive movement forwards.

"Stay back!" Nubi snapped at Tyson. "You cannot help him! It was decided that he should be the one to face the tessst, and he mussst do it alone. Otherwise you forfeit your chance for the puppiesss lives!"

Tyson bristled and looked worriedly at Max, but he stayed where he was.

They circled again—Max and the creature—and shifted their weight, each waiting for the other to strike first. They were by the river now, sandwiched between the dark water rushing past and one of the gigantic pillars rising out of the floor of the hall. Ammut lashed her tail suddenly and charged at Max. He dodged, but the creature kept after him relentlessly, whipping around and around, jaws snapping.

Honey felt fear choke in her throat like a stuck bone as she watched Max scrabble to keep out of range. He was limping now and leaving a trail of blood behind him. He swerved one more time, but not fast enough, and that powerful crocodile tail swung through the air and smacked into him, flinging him towards the stone pillar.

"MAX!" Honey yelped as she saw the Pit Bull's body slam against the pillar, then crumple to the ground beneath.

Max opened his eyes and shook his head. He raised himself up on his forepaws, panting, then struggled painfully to his feet. Ammut grunted and began moving towards him, but she was slow and there was still time to get away.

So why wasn't Max moving?

"What's he doing?" whispered Suka.

"Go! GO! You can still get away!" cried Honey, staring at Max.

But the Pit Bull didn't move. He remained in front of the pillar and watched Ammut approaching, a glint in his eyes. The monster roared—a triumphant note this time—and Nubi laughed gleefully. Then Ammut lowered her head and charged.

CHAPTER 30

For a moment, everything seemed to slow down and all Honey could hear was the pounding of her heart and blood rushing with a deafening roar in her ears. She saw Ammut's legs moving, gaining speed as the creature rushed towards the stone pillar, eyes fixed on Max. Those lethal jaws flashed open, aiming for Max, but just before the teeth closed around him, the Pit Bull dived sideways, rolling over in the sand. Ammut's jaws smashed into the pillar and embedded themselves into the stone.

The creature roared and thrashed, but the force of her charge had pushed her fangs too far into the stone. Her head was immobilised. She screamed and lashed her tail, scraping the stone in vain as she struggled to free herself.

Then with a sudden heave backwards, Ammut pulled herself loose. A shower of stone burst from the pillar as she smashed her way out, leaving a hole that spread upwards in great cracks towards the ceiling.

But the force with which she had pulled herself free was her undoing. Ammut reeled back, the momentum causing her to fall over. She slipped and rolled into the river.

She submerged.

Then her head appeared again. But something was wrong. She was disorientated, turning her head blindly. Her tail lashed through the water as she heaved herself over in a frenzy of rolls, trying to regain the shore.

But the water was too fast, too furious.

It carried her, still screaming and thrashing, down the river, past the boat containing the puppies, and over the waterfall. Her screams echoed hollowly, then faded into the abyss.

"No!" snarled Nubi, his eyes disbelieving. "*No!*" A howl of fury rose from deep in his chest. The flesh seemed to shrink away from his skull so that his face looked like a dog mask with empty eyes. The howl rose to a shriek which whirled around him like a cyclone, turning him into a blur of black fur.

Then he was gone. The echo of his howl faded away to the corners of the great hall.

The dogs stared at each other.

"Howling hyenas, he did it!" said Suka, her blue eyes round. "Max totally did it!"

"Max won!" Ruffster barked, jumping up and down.

"*A-woo-woo-woo-woo!*" howled Biscuit, running in circles.

"Max!" Honey whirled around. "You saved the puppies! You..." She faltered as she saw the shape slumped on the ground. "Max?"

They rushed towards him and Honey leaned over, her heart clenching in fear. She shoved her nose into the blood-soaked fur. "Max? Max?"

The Pit Bull turned glazed eyes towards her. His breathing was harsh and laboured, each breath seeming to wrench itself out of his chest. A dark red pool was spreading around him. He moved a paw slightly and Honey saw his tail give a feeble wag.

"Don't... don't... think... I'll be... coming back... with you," he panted.

"No, Max, no..." Honey whimpered, crouching down next to him. The other dogs huddled around, pressing close, their eyes shocked.

"My... Old Man...," he gasped, "...hope he can... understand... why... I didn't... come home..."

Honey nuzzled Max's face, feeling his breath weakening. "Why, Max?" she said desperately. "Why did you do it? You knew! You knew that your heart—"

Max touched his nose to hers. Behind the glaze of pain, she saw a smile in his eyes. "What good... is a heart... if you... cannot... give it away? You... showed me that." His tail gave another feeble wag, and his chest rose and fell one last time. Then he was gone.

Suka sat up slowly and raised her nose to the sky. She let out a long, mournful Husky howl that rose and echoed through the hall. Biscuit raised his nose and added his hound voice too.

"I was wrong about him," said Tyson

quietly, looking down at Max.

"We were all wrong about him, mate," said Ruffster.

Honey just stared. She couldn't believe it. Max looked so peaceful. Like he was sleeping. Like he could wake up any moment. She shoved her nose into his neck. His fur was soft and still warm. She ignored the others as they tried to push her away. But then she heard something else that she couldn't ignore. An ominous rumbling. The ground beneath her paws began to shake.

She raised her head from Max's body. The others were staggering around, trying to keep their footing. Something crashed to the ground next to Honey, narrowly missing her. A chunk of stone. More chunks began raining down from the sky.

"What—?"

"The pillar!" Ruffster cried, looking towards the giant pillar Ammut had smashed into. "It's breakin'! The whole place is fallin' apart!"

Honey sprang up. He was right. The pillar was collapsing in on itself, crumbling in swirls of dust. High above, where it must have joined to the ceiling of the hall, the cracking stone was spreading. Jagged chasms split across the whole ceiling, loosening chunks of stone that plummeted down to smash against the ground. The other pillars began shaking as well.

"We've got to get out of here!" Suka yelped.

"The puppies!" cried Honey. "What about them?"

She looked towards the boat. What she saw made her heart drop to her paws. The boat was straining tight against its rope, bucking and heaving on the water, which had swelled into furious waves. Huge chunks of stone were raining down from the ceiling and falling into the river with mighty splashes that sent small tsunamis surging forwards, each one slamming into the boat with greater force and soaking the puppies inside. They were awake now and their eyes were wide with fright as they huddled together. Every time the boat rolled and rocked, they were thrown from side to side.

"Bean!" cried Honey as she saw the Dane pup tumbling to the side of the boat. For a heart-stopping moment, she thought Bean would go over the side, but the Dane puppy grabbed on to the wooden edge of the boat with her teeth and clung on. Her terrified whimper reached Honey's ears.

"Hang on! I'm coming!" Honey scrambled forwards, slipping in the sand.

The others followed and they bounded towards the boat. But they stopped in consternation as they reached the shore. The boat was no longer moored alongside the bank—the rushing water had forced it further out into the middle of the river so that the dogs couldn't reach it unless they swam out. The only thing keeping the boat from floating down the river and going over the edge of the abyss was the thin stretch of rope attached to the post on the bank. But even as they watched, another surging wave heaved the boat up and almost rolled it over.

The rope stretched even more. Frayed. Then snapped.

The boat with the puppies whirled in the waves and began drifting down the river, towards the edge of the abyss.

CHAPTER 31

Someone rushed past Honey and sprang into the air. It was Ruffster, twisting his body in an impossible leap—just as she had seen him do so many times at the park when he had chased after his Frisbee. His neck stretched out and he grabbed at something in the air. His legs thrashed as he plummeted downwards, and for one horrible second, Honey thought he would drop into the water. Then he landed at the edge of the river, his paws scrabbling on the shore, his teeth clamped around the rope.

The boat jerked to a stop again and wobbled in the currents. More puppies cried out, whimpering and shivering, but at least they were all still in the boat. Ruffster strained against the rope as he heaved himself back up the bank, fighting against the force of the rushing water.

"Hang on, Ruffster!"

Honey jumped forwards and grabbed the rope with her teeth as well. Together with Ruffster, she pulled, harder than she had ever pulled in her life. Her legs slipped and skidded and she braced them to stop herself sliding into the river. The rope strained between her teeth, cutting into the soft skin of her jowls, but she held on. It was like the hardest game of Tug she had ever played.

Then slowly, slowly, she felt the boat coming. She shifted backwards, still pulling, and felt Ruffster move with her. Another heave. And another. Together, they dragged the boat slowly out of the river and onto the bank until it was clear of the water. Honey dropped the rope, gasping and panting as water dripped from her ears, nose, and chin.

"Whew!" said Ruffster, shaking himself vigorously. "Thought I was goin' on a one-way trip to *Duat* for a minute there."

Suka, Tyson, and Biscuit crowded around the boat, sniffing the puppies inside.

"They look OK!" said Suka, wagging her tail. "I thought—"

Another ominous rumble sounded at the far end of the hall.

CRACK!

A sound like thunder echoed on this side and a sudden chasm appeared in the ground beside them.

"Look out!"

More chunks of stone crashed to the ground around them. The dogs staggered and lurched as the ground beneath their feet dipped and shifted.

"Quick! The tunnel! Get back to the tunnel!" yelled Ruffster.

"What about the puppies?" Honey looked

desperately at the bedraggled pile of puppies in the boat. *Could they carry them all out in time?* She reached into the boat to grab the closest puppy by its scruff.

"Wait!" Suka jumped forwards. "I've got an idea!"

The Husky grabbed the end of the rope in her mouth and rolled over several times, squirming and turning so that when she stood up, the rope was wrapped around her chest and body. *Like a harness*! Honey realised.

Suka walked to the end of the rope until it was taut, then threw herself forwards and pulled. It was a powerful, instinctive movement that echoed right back to her Husky ancestors in the Arctic. Suka might never have led a sled team across the snows, but pulling was in her blood. Everyone held their breath as she strained, rigid against the rope. Then the boat began sliding forwards across the ground.

"Holy liver treat! You're doin' it, Suka!"

Suka heaved again, throwing all her weight into the rope, then began walking faster. She broke into a trot and the boat bumped across the sand after her. The Husky raced towards the tunnel, pulling the boat behind her like a sled.

"*A-woo-woo-woo!*" barked Biscuit, chasing after her.

"C'mon!" Ruffster urged, following Tyson towards the tunnel.

"Wait! What about Max?" Honey cried, looking back towards the huddle of fur on the ground.

"There's no time!"

"No, I'm not leaving him!" Honey turned and ran back to Max's body. "We need to take him back... so his Old Man isn't left wondering. We can't just leave him here!"

"Festerin' fleas, Honey—you crazy?" Ruffster spluttered, stopping at mouth of the tunnel and looking back at her.

Honey ignored him. She reached down to grab Max by the scruff at the back of his neck. His body was heavy. She managed to drag it for a few feet, then had to stop, panting. Something sharp struck her face. She shook her head as she felt the warm trickle of blood. A piece of stone had hit her, leaving a gash above her eye. All around her, she could feel more chunks of stone crashing down. *I'll never make it!* She took a deep breath and fought the panic rising in her throat. *But I'm not leaving Max.* She reached down again.

Then someone was pulling along with her, easing the load. She looked up in surprise. It was Tyson. The Jack Russell had come back to help her! He wagged his tail and she touched his nose gratefully. Together, they pulled and dragged Max's body across the hall and into the tunnel. Many of the flaming logs were burning out now, plunging sections of the tunnel into darkness, but they kept going. Honey could feel her teeth aching from their grip on Max's fur and next to her, she saw Tyson's muscles quivering as he struggled to keep pulling. but neither of them let go.

Another bend. Then another. Then something tickled her nostrils.

Fresh air!

Honey looked up. They were near the end of the tunnel and above them, at the top of the steps, was the open *Ka* door. The boat had jammed at the bottom of the steps but Ruffster, Suka, and Biscuit were grabbing the puppies and carrying them out one by one, as fast as they could. Bean was the last one left in the boat now. Suka struggled as she tried to pick the Dane puppy up by the scruff. She heaved and staggered, then gave up and just nudged Bean up the steps as quickly as she could.

"Honey! Tyson!" Ruffster wagged his tail. "We were just goin' back to look for you!"

He jumped forwards and helped them pull Max's body up the steps and over the rim of the *Ka* door. Honey scrambled out last. Below, in the tunnel behind them, they heard more rumbling and crashing. The stone slab shuddered.

"Quick! Get off! Get off the door!" Ruffster shouted.

Honey grabbed Bean and jumped off the stone slab just as the central section swung back into place with a creaking groan. Dust puffed as the edges sealed shut. The earth around the stone slab shook as it seemed to sink deeper into the ground, and soon most of its surface was covered by soil again. The *Ka* door shuddered once more, then was silent.

Honey raised her head and looked around.

Moonlight flooded the cemetery, lingering over the rows of tombstones in the distance and washing over the silhouettes of her friends around her as well as the limp huddle of Max's body. Then Honey felt her heart lighten as the pale glow lit up a dozen little faces huddled together. The puppies. They had brought them back home.

CHAPTER 32

It was late afternoon—the time when most dogs like to walk their humans. The sun hovered low in the sky, bathing everything in a golden light as Honey turned the corner of the street beside the park. It was hard to believe that only last night she had stood in a deserted cemetery filled with shadows and nightmares.

She caught sight of Ruffster and paused to wait for him to join her.

"How's the pup doin'?" he asked.

Honey looked over her shoulder at Bean scampering behind her. Perhaps she had been a little less bouncy this morning, but now the Dane puppy seemed to be tackling things with her usual boisterous gusto... including trying to eat the lamp post. Again.

"She seems OK," Honey said, her voice low. "I don't think she really remembers what happened. Those scarabs kept the puppies pretty woozy. The bite on her paw should heal over soon. Maybe she'll just think it was all a bad dream."

"Worst dream I've ever had," muttered Ruffster, shaking his head.

"Look, Wuffta, I have ouchie," said Bean, bouncing up to Ruffster and showing him her paw. A pale pink swelling with a puncture hole in the middle showed clearly, like the bite from a giant tick.

"Yeah, me too," said Ruffster, turning to show Bean his shoulder, which sported a long gash. A memento from where a chunk of the stone pillar had hit him. "Don't worry, pup, yours will heal up soon. Reckon you'll have a cool scar to show off to everybody."

"Scar!" Bean bounced excitedly and ran off ahead of them.

Ruffster turned back to Honey. "You get away from the Pet Sitter OK? Didn't think she'd let you out o' her sight now."

"Yeah, you should have seen her when I brought Bean home. I didn't think she'd stop crying. But don't worry, I've picked up a few tricks from Suka," Honey said, grinning. Then she sobered. "Anyway, this is important."

Ruffster nodded and they turned together into Lemon Tree Lane. Down at the bottom were the gates to the cemetery, standing open. And next to the cemetery stood a house surrounded by a high hedge. Honey felt her heart constrict. *Max's house.*

A voice called behind them. Honey turned to see Tyson coming slowly towards them from the other end of the main street. He was panting heavily as he dragged something along the ground with him. As he got closer, they saw that it was a huge marrow bone, the ends crusted with fresh soil. Everyone knew Tyson kept the best bone stash in town—dogs whispered constantly about the treasures buried in his garden—but he always kept it a closely guarded secret. Honey couldn't believe she was finally seeing a piece of the Jack Russell's famous collection. The smell of the bone was incredible. She licked her jowls hastily to hide the drool.

"Holy liver treat!" Ruffster said, his nose twitching. "Is that from a dinosaur or somethin'?"

"It's one of my 2009 batch. Well-rotted. Fishy, with a hint of cabbage. Sharp on the nose but rich in texture," growled Tyson. He met Honey's eyes. "It's... er... a gift."

She wagged her tail gently. "I'm sure he would have loved it."

Bean scampered over to inspect the bone too. "Yummy?"

"Yes, but not for ya," growled Tyson.

"Why?"

"Because yer too young to appreciate such things."

"Why?"

The Jack Russell gave an impatient grunt. "Because ya still got to grow—"

"Am big girl now!" shouted Bean, bouncing around Tyson. "You smaller!"

Honey winced. At ten weeks, the Dane puppy *was* already taller than Tyson, her knuckly paws almost as big as his head. But the last thing you wanted to do was point that out to a Jack Russell! Hastily, she nudged Bean away from her fuming friend and started to hustle her down Lemon Tree Lane, towards the cemetery.

"Um... Honey...?"

Honey looked back. Tyson was standing next to the bone, not quite meeting her eyes.

"Um... do ya think ya can help me?" he said stiffly. "It's... it's a bit tough for a... *er*... smaller dog to manage."

"What?" Ruffster stared. "Did you just call yourself a small—"

"Of course I can help you," said Honey quickly as Tyson glared at Ruffster. "I'm sure any sized dog would need help with this." She grabbed one end of the marrow bone and started dragging it along. Together, she and Tyson manoeuvred it to the gates of the cemetery, where Biscuit and Suka met them.

"Oh my Dog!" said Biscuit, his eyes boggling. "Is that a Marrow Blanc 2009?" He shoved his nose into the bone and sniffed reverently, licking his chops.

"Keep yer nose to yerself," growled Tyson, edging the bone away. "It's not for ya."

"Hey, I'm just having a sniff. What's the harm in—"

The creaking of a garden gate caught their attention. A figure emerged from between the high hedge around Max's house and stepped out onto the lane. They watched as he walked towards them. It was the Old Man carrying a bundle in his arms. A larger bundle this time, which he held tenderly, tucking the blanket carefully around it. He smiled slightly at them as he approached and they parted to let him enter the cemetery. Silently, they followed him in.

In the warm, golden light of the afternoon, the cemetery looked nothing like the sinister place of last night. A gentle breeze rustled through the tall grass and birds called softly in the branches above. As they approached the area of the pet memorials, Honey glanced over to the far corner, but the *Ka* door was hardly noticeable, looking like nothing more now than a worn slab of stone, half buried beneath the ground. Already weeds were sprouting through the disturbed earth.

It's over. She shook her head and turned back to look at the bundle in the Old Man's arms. *And now it's time to say goodbye.*

A fresh section of the ground had been cleared next to the path. The Old Man walked over and laid his bundle gently in the shallow hole. Honey and her friends clustered around and bowed their heads. Even Bean stopped bouncing and sat solemnly next to Honey, her eyes wide.

"Scary doggie?" asked Bean. "Scary doggie sleeping?"

"Yes," said Honey. "But not 'scary' doggie. Brave doggie. He gave his life for you and the other puppies."

The Old Man said something softly—too soft for Honey to hear—then reached out to stroke the bundle one last time. Tyson stood up and began pushing the marrow bone with his nose until it rolled into the hole next to the bundle. The Old Man smiled and reached out to pat Tyson.

"Thank you." He stood up and began to gently cover the bundle with fresh earth.

Soon there was a small mound where the bundle had been. Each of the dogs walked over and placed a paw on the mound, leaving a paw print in the soft soil. Honey was last. She hesitated, not wanting to do it, not wanting to admit that he was really gone.

"Brave doggie gone?" asked Bean.

Honey placed her paw firmly down on the mound. A perfect paw print. Like the one he had left on her heart.

"No," she said softly to Bean. "He's not gone."

"Why?"

"Because... he will always be with us, in our hearts," said Honey.

A loud whistle made them all look up. A young man was hurrying in through the gates of the cemetery, chasing a black puppy that ran ahead of him. Honey's heart skipped a beat. The big head on the scrawny neck. The short, stubby legs. The whiskery chin. She knew this puppy. He ran up to them and bounced around Bean, who squealed in delight and threw herself on him. In a minute, the two puppies were tumbling over on the ground, laughing and wrestling with each other.

"You've been adopted?" Honey asked, wagging her tail in delight.

"Yes! Yesterday!" The black puppy jumped up to lick her face. "I've got a Forever Home!" He looked back towards the young man who was peering around the tombstones. "That's my new human. He's nice. D'you know what he said? He told the pet-shop people I'm not ugly. He said I have 'character'."

"He's right," said Honey giving the puppy a lick, adding softly to herself, *And Nubi was wrong... there are some humans who can choose with their hearts.*

"Me Bean!" said Bean, bashing the black puppy with one giant paw. "Who you?"

The black puppy looked a bit crestfallen. "My human hasn't picked a name for me yet. This is our first walk! He said maybe it will help him think of a name for me." He looked up at Honey. "Do you have an idea for a name?"

Honey looked over to the mound where the Old Man was carefully depositing a memorial stone, its surface etched with a name and a message. She turned back to the puppy. "What about Max? That's a good name."

"Why?" asked the black puppy and Bean together.

"I knew a dog named Max," said Honey softly. "He was the bravest dog I've ever known. And he was my friend. Any dog would be proud to carry his name."

"But—"

"There you are!" The young man arrived, huffing and puffing, to join them. He was sweating and his face was red, but his eyes were kind. The black puppy scampered back to him, bouncing around his legs. The young man laughed and reached down to pat his puppy, then he paused as he caught sight of the Old Man. Honey saw the smile fade from his face. He stood up and walked quietly over to where the Old Man stood, looking down at Max's grave.

Honey watched as the two men stood there for a long time without saying anything. Nearby, the two puppies yipped and squealed as they rolled around, play-fighting. Finally, the young man reached out and laid a hand on the Old Man's shoulder. Then he pointed to the memorial stone and bent his head to say something. The Old Man nodded. Honey held her breath, hope surging in her chest.

The young man turned around and crouched down, holding his hands out to the black puppy.

"Max! Here, boy!"

The black puppy barked excitedly as he ran over to the young man. Honey felt her heart lift. She glanced back at the mound, then smiled to herself as she thought of what she had told Bean. *No, Max was not gone.*

"Howling hyenas, I'd better get back home or I'll end up in the doghouse," said Suka, leading the way back out of the cemetery. She turned to Biscuit. "Hey, I'm going with my Boy to the school fair today. I heard my Boy's Mother talking about your Missus. Maybe you guys are coming along too."

"Will there be food?" asked Biscuit, trotting hopefully after her.

Tyson snorted in disgust and trailed after them.

"Reckon my Guy will be lookin' for me too by now," said Ruffster, stopping to cock his leg against a bush. "What about you, Honey?

Isn't your Olivia back soon?"

"Not 'til the end of the week," said Honey, watching Bean bounce ahead of them. Suddenly she didn't mind the thought of sharing her home with the puppy anymore. It might be really nice, she thought, imagining long, peaceful afternoons while she snoozed in the sun with the puppy curled up next to her. After everything that had happened, life was going to be easy now, filled with—

She stepped into something soft and squishy. *What was that awful smell?*

Honey looked down in horror as Bean bounced around her.

The Dane pup wagged her tail proudly. "I poo!"

THE END

Thank you for reading this book. If you enjoyed the story, please do tell your friends and consider leaving a review on Amazon, even if it's just a few lines—it would be greatly appreciated! Thank you!

Look out for Honey's next adventure Coming soon in late 2014!

Sign up for the newsletter at:
www.bighoneydogmysteries.com
to be notified of new releases, get sneak previews and enter special members-only competitions.

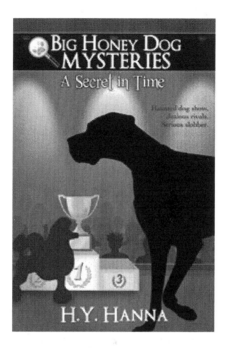

BIG HONEY DOG MYSTERIES #2:
A SECRET IN TIME

Haunted dog show.
Jealous rivals.
Serious slobber.

When Honey the Great Dane arrives at a dog show, the last thing she expects to meet is her doggie doppelgänger! But things get even stranger when her famous 'twin' is poisoned and Honey is asked to take her place in the show ring... She soon finds that the glamorous world of champions hides some ugly secrets. Are the Showgrounds really haunted by a Phantom Hound? What really happened ten years ago when a mysterious fire claimed two lives? And just how far will someone go to win the title of 'Best in Show'?

PRAISE FOR THE BIG HONEY DOG MYSTERIES:

"I've read a few books marketed for middle-grades or younger this year and I have to say that this is hands down the best suited for those ages. It has a great plot, some truly well-rounded characters (with more depth than what I find in most adult novels these days) and a climax that will keep you on the edge of your seat."- LitChick Hit List

"If you want to get your middle grade reader interested in picking up books, then this is a great place to start." - Net Galley reviewer

"The author has a great voice with a wonderful sense of humour." - Indie Abode Book Reviews

"We are loving this book. My 10 year old son who has a short attention span cannot get enough." – Net Galley reviewer

Available as EBOOK and PAPERBACK from Amazon and other online bookstores, as well as by order from your local bookshop.

BIG HONEY DOG MYSTERIES
Christmas Special Edition:
MESSAGE IN A BAUBLE

Christmas intrigue.
Daring rescue.
Serious slobber.

When Honey the Great Dane finds a hidden note inside a strange Christmas bauble, the happy festive season turns ominous. Was the note from a trapped child? Join Honey and her canine friends as they set off on a daring Search & Rescue - in a mystery filled with candy canes, gingerbread cookies and lots of mince pies!

Available as EBOOK from Amazon and
other online bookstores

**BIG HONEY DOG MYSTERIES Easter
Special Edition:
TREASURE FROM THE PAST**

*Long-lost heirloom.
Desperate egg hunt.
Serious slobber.*

Join Honey the Great Dane and her canine friends in this exciting Easter mystery as they come across a strange, fairy-tale house and its mysterious occupants. Can they decipher the clues in time to find a priceless lost treasure from the Russian Revolution?

Available as EBOOK from Amazon and other online bookstores

ABOUT THE AUTHOR

H.Y. Hanna is Taiwanese by birth, British by education, pseudo-American by accent and now Australian by residence! After graduating from Oxford University, she tried her hand at a variety of jobs before returning to her first love: writing. Hsin-Yi has always been searching for close encounters of the canine kind. Where other girls grew up pony-mad, Hsin-Yi was dog-mad: her favourite bedtime reading was the Encyclopaedia of Dog Breeds and her favourite activity was practising a really authentic bark.

When she wasn't doing Rottweiler impressions, Hsin-Yi spent her time devouring mysteries. Her childhood idol was Nancy Drew - not just because Nancy could scuba dive, speak French, sell insurance and solve mysteries - often all at the same time - but also because Hsin-Yi really wanted "strawberry-blonde hair". When she's not working on her next novel, she's usually found watching repeats of her favourite TV show, Fringe, or wiping Dane slobber off the walls.

You can write to Hsin-Yi and find out more about her (and the 'real-life Honey' who inspired the series) at:

www.bighoneydogmysteries.com,—

where you'll also find fun activity sheets and interactive puzzles, as well as book discussion questions and other parent/teacher resources. Or follow her on the **Big Honey Dog Mysteries Facebook Page**—and become a fan to keep up with all the latest news and updates!

ACKNOWLEDGEMENTS

This book would not have been possible without the help and support of so many wonderful people. First, a *huge* thank you to Melanie G Howe who not only read and critiqued every chapter and rewrite of the first draft but also endured endless emails discussing plot holes and character development, provided a shoulder to cry on and an ear to vent to, held my hand and knocked some common sense into my head when I succumbed to writers' blues and is just an all-round, amazing friend. Melanie—I could not have done this without you.

Thank you also to my lovely friend, Nicoletta Baschirotto, for her enthusiasm, support and help, especially with all the hard work researching a character which sadly never made it into the final draft (but might hopefully appear in a future book of the series!). And to my long-time 'BFFs', Shir-Hwa Ueng and Basma Alwesh for always thinking of me, even from halfway across the world.

A very special thanks goes out to my

fantastic group of beta readers for their feedback and insights which have helped me make the story the best it can be: Anastasia Tureson, Emily Sharapan, Kaitlyn Egan, Leni Schrader, Mackenzie Peña-Martinez, Margeaux Denning-Duke, Mark & Ryan McDonald, Charlotte Howgego, Delaney Roberson, McKenzie Ross, Carmel Downey, Robin Trott and the students at Glacial Hills Elementary School, Starbuck, MN, and Paige Whitley and her boys, Jack, Max, Sam & Noah. Also, to Cristy Burne and my writing group for their help with the crucial opening chapters.

To the team who helped make this book a reality: Anne Victory, Kim Killion and Jennifer Jakes – thank you for your skills, patience with me and efforts to accommodate my publishing schedule. Thank you also to Dr. Mark-Jan Nederhof for allowing me to use his beautiful hieroglyphic scripts to help tell the story. And to my agent, Dorothy Lumley, for being one of the first to believe in me.

To all our blog friends and fans of Honey's blog—thank you for following us through the years and sharing this journey with us. Your comments, support and enthusiasm mean more to me than I can say and have motivated me and encouraged me every step of the way. Here's to many more exciting adventures together!

I'd also like to mention my wonderful mother, Ma-Ma, and my siblings and extended family through marriage—though we are often separated by great distances, your support and encouragement have always meant a lot to me.

And last but not least to my amazing husband, Paul, who is the most incredible man (and not just because he picks up my socks!) —I would not be where I am now without him and his unwavering support and constant belief in me. To Honey for always making me smile, even in my darkest hours; to Lemon for being the first and to Muesli— because I can't not mention that little tabby princess, even though I don't know what she's done, really, except steal my chair at every opportunity!

Made in the USA
Lexington, KY
14 September 2014